The Tragic Pursuit of Being

THE TRAGIC PURSUIT
OF BEING

Unamuno and Sartre

ROBERT RICHMOND ELLIS

THE UNIVERSITY OF ALABAMA PRESS

Tuscaloosa and London

Copyright © 1988 by
The University of Alabama Press
Tuscaloosa, Alabama 35487
All rights reserved
Manufactured in the United States of America

Library of Congress Cataloging-in-Publication Data

Ellis, Robert Richmond.
  The tragic pursuit of being.

  Bibliography: p.
  Includes index.
  1. Sartre, Jean Paul, 1905–   —Criticism and interpretation. 2. Unamuno, Miguel de, 1864–1936—Criticism
and interpretation. 3. Existentialism in literature.
4. Existentialism. 5. Literature, Comparative—French
and Spanish. 6. Literature, Comparative—Spanish and
French. I. Title.
PQ2637.A82Z67 1988   848'.91409   87-18209
ISBN 0-8173-0385-5

British Library Cataloguing-in-Publication Data is available.

Contents

Acknowledgments

The following permissions are acknowledged:

Jean-Paul Sartre, *Being and Nothingness: A Phenomenological Essay on Ontology*. Translated and with introduction by Hazel E. Barnes. Copyright © 1956 by Philosophical Library, Inc. Reprinted by permission of Philosophical Library, Inc. (USA and Canada) and Methuen & Company, Ltd. (UK and Commonwealth).

Jean-Paul Sartre, *Critique of Dialectical Reason 1:* Theory of Practical Ensembles. Translated by Alan Sheridan-Smith. Edited by Jonathan Ree. Copyright © 1976 by NLB. Reprinted by permission of Verso/NLB.

Jean-Paul Sartre, *Nausea.* Translated by Lloyd Alexander. Introduction by Hayden Carruth. Copyright © 1964 by New Directions Publishing Corporation. Reprinted by permission of New Directions Publishing Corporation.

Jean-Paul Sartre, *What Is Literature?* Translated by Bernard Frechtman. Copyright © 1949 by Philosophical Library, Inc. Reprinted by permission of Philosophical Library, Inc.

Miguel de Unamuno y Jugo, *Selected Works of Miguel de Unamuno*, Bollingen Series, LXXXV, Vol. 4: *The Tragic Sense of Life in Men and Nations.* Translated by Anthony Kerrigan. Introduction by Salvador de Madariaga. Afterword by William Barrett. Copyright © 1972 by Princeton University Press. Reprinted by permission of Princeton University Press (USA, Canada, and Open Market) and Routledge & Kegan Paul (UK and Commonwealth).

Miguel de Unamuno y Jugo, *Selected Works of Miguel de Unamuno*, Bollingen Series LXXXV, Vol. 5: *The Agony of Christianity and Essays on Faith.* Translated by Anthony Kerrigan. Annotated by Martin Nozick and Anthony Kerrigan. Copyright © 1974 by Princeton University Press. Reprinted by permission of Princeton University Press (USA, Canada, and Open Market) and Routledge & Kegan Paul (UK and Commonwealth).

Miguel de Unamuno y Jugo, *Selected Works of Miguel de Unamuno*, Bollingen Series LXXXV, Vol. 6: *Novela/Nivola.* Translated and with introduction by Anthony Kerrigan. Copyright © 1976 by Princeton University Press. Reprinted by permission of Princeton University Press (USA, Canada, and Open Market) and Routledge and Kegan Paul (UK and Commonwealth).

Miguel de Unamuno y Jugo, *Selected Works of Miguel de Unamuno*, Bollingen Series LXXXV, Vol. 7: *Ficciones: Four Stories and a Play.* Translated by Anthony Kerrigan. Introduction and notes by Martin Nozick. Copyright © 1976 by Princeton University Press. Reprinted by permission of Princeton Uni-

Preface

Miguel de Unamuno is modern Spain's most enigmatic intellectual figure. More critical scholarship has been devoted to his work than to that of any Spanish writer of the twentieth century. Yet the same question is repeatedly raised: What is its ultimate meaning? It is a question that leads us to the heart of the most profound philosophical and literary problems of our day. If we are to answer it, we must first ask ourselves a practical question: Do we possess at this moment in history a methodology capable of broaching a thought as diverse and as complex as Unamuno's? Is there a key?

In his studies of Genet and Flaubert, Sartre has revealed the heuristic nature of the methodological approach of existentialism. Rather than re-articulate its fundamental premises through a study of man, existentialism takes man as an absolute end. For this reason it is a humanism. Existentialism holds that man not only raises the fundamental question of human reality but that he provides, through an original ontological choice, the answer. It is existentialism, therefore, that will reveal the "truth" of Unamuno. Through it we will gain something we did not possess at the outset, and in the end our effort will be justified.

An existentialist approach to the work of Unamuno is particularly appropriate in light of the fact that Unamuno was, in the profound sense of the term, an existentialist. It has become common practice among certain scholars of Spanish letters to regard Unamuno as a precursor of the existentialist movement and in particular of Sartre. Nevertheless, while Unamuno's essays and literature contain the insights that Sartre would theorize in his philosophical treatises, no dialogue existed between the two thinkers. Unamuno was born a generation be-

ix

fore Sartre and was unfamiliar with his work. While Sartre knew of the work of Unamuno, he mentions him only once. This reference appears in the introduction to the *Critique of Dialectical Reason*. Here, Sartre contrasts his realist philosophy with what he considers to be Unamuno's idealism: "We rejected the official idealism in the name of 'the tragic sense of life.'"[1] In a footnote he clarifies his statement: "This phrase was made popular by the Spanish philosopher Miguel de Unamuno. Of course, this tragic sense had nothing in common with the true conflicts of our period."[2]

This categorical pronouncement must lay to rest once and for all the claim critics might make regarding the question of Unamuno as a precursor of Sartre. It nevertheless reveals a misunderstanding on the part of Sartre. Unamuno was not, as Sartre suggests, a true philosopher nor was his vision of the world, strictly speaking, idealistic. When asked by colleagues why he chose not to create a philosophical system, Unamuno argued that systematized thought becomes an ideology that enchains the freedom on which it is founded. Much like Kierkegaard, he rejected formal philosophy, and though his thought is profoundly "philosophical," he took existence rather than knowledge as both his point of departure and his end. It is precisely for this reason that Unamuno is a central figure in what might be called the "existentialist revolution" of the late nineteenth and early twentieth centuries.

Unamuno's rejection of philosophy raises a question central to existentialism itself. How is an intuition of existence to be communicated to others if it cannot, in the final analysis, be made an object of knowledge? Is the intuition somehow mistaken or is language simply incapable of elucidating the fundamental structures of existence? What Unamuno would discover was the inadequacy of rational discourse. It is for this reason that he would make literature his primary means of expression and at the end of his life would state that his entire work was essentially that of a poet.[3]

What, then, is the relationship between a man who chooses to identify himself as a poet and one who utters in private: *"La littérature, . . . c'est de la merde"*?[4] The answer to this question is to be found in a fundamental existential intui-

x

tion which the two thinkers share. While Sartre claims to reject Unamuno's articulation of the tragic sense of life, we are astounded at his words in the recently published *Morale* which speak of consciousness in terms of the "tragedy of the pursuit of being."[5] Both Unamuno and Sartre find tragedy at the core of the human experience. They differ, however, in the choice they make regarding the meaning of tragedy.

Because Unamuno refused to establish a systematic philosophy, many of his readers are baffled by his work. With the instruments provided by the completed Sartrean system, however, we are now in a position to undertake a new reading of Unamuno and to articulate his "unwritten philosophy." In this way his work will be made available to the reader with a clarity which it has heretofore lacked. Ultimately we will be able to place the question regarding the relationship between Unamuno and Sartre in its final perspective.

What we will learn is that Unamuno's work reveals the pre-reflective, lived-moment of the human condition while Sartre's expresses the passage of that moment to reflexivity. Through the juxtaposition of their two *oeuvres* we will thus discover both the "meaning" of Unamuno and the "heart" of Sartre. In the process we will come to know and feel the existential experience of modern man. To use the words of Sartre in his study of Genet, the world we are about to enter is like a mirror held up to us: "We must look at it and see ourselves."[6]

Chronology

Unamuno

1864   Born September 29 in Bilbao

1870   Father dies

1880   Completes secondary studies and enters the Faculty of Philosophy and Letters of the University of Madrid

1883   Receives licentiate degree

1884   Begins a philosophical tract based on Hegelian thought titled *Logical Philosophy (Filosofía lógica)*

Completes university courses and takes a degree in Philosophy and Letters with a major in language

Submits a dissertation titled *Critical Study of the Problem of the Origins and Prehistory of the Basque Race (Crítica del problema sobre el origen y prehistoria de la raza vasca)*

1891   Obtains a chair in Greek at the University of Salamanca

Marries Concepción Lizárraga, with whom he will have nine children

1894   Enrolls in the Bilbao branch of the Socialist Party

1895   Writes the essays which will comprise *On Authentic Tradition (En torno al casticismo)*

1896   Third son Raimundo fatally stricken with meningitis

1897   Experiences first and most profound religious crisis

Publishes first novel *Peace in War (Paz en la guerra)*

1898   Writes the play *The Sphinx (La esfinge)*

1899   Reads the essay *Nicodemus the Pharisee (Nicodemo el fariseo)* in the Atheneum of Madrid

Publishes the essay *On University Teaching in Spain (De la enseñanza superior en España)* and writes the play *The Blindfold (La venda)*

1900   Named rector of the University of Salamanca

Begins to read Kierkegaard
Publishes the essays *Ideocracy (La ideocracia), Go Within! (¡Adentro!)*, and *Faith (La fe)*
1902 Publishes the essays of *On Authentic Tradition*, the travel sketches *Landscapes (Paisajes)*, and the novel *Love and Education (Amor y pedagogía)*
1903 Publishes *From My Native Region (De mi país)*
1905 Publishes *The Life of Don Quijote and Sancho (La vida de Don Quijote y Sancho)*
1907 Publishes first book of poetry, titled *Poems (Poesías)*
1908 Publishes *Memories of Childhood and Adolescence (Recuerdos de niñez y mocedad)*
Mother dies
1910 Publishes *My Religion and Other Short Essays (Mi religión y otros ensayos breves)*
Writes the play *Fedra*
1911 Publishes *Through Regions of Portugal and Spain (Por tierras de Portugal y España), Soliloquies and Conversations (Soliloquios y conversaciones)*, and *Rosary of Lyrical Sonnets (Rosario de sonetos líricos)*
1912 Publishes *Against This and That (Contra esto y aquello)*
1913 Publishes the philosophical treatise *On the Tragic Sense of Life in Men and Nations (Del sentimiento trágico de la vida en los hombres y en los pueblos)*
1914 Publishes the novel *Mist (Niebla)*
Dismissed from the rectorship of the University of Salamanca because of attacks against the Germanophile Alfonso XIII and the Spanish government
1916 Writes a prologue to Ramón Turró's *Origins of Knowledge: Hunger (Orígenes del conocimiento: El hambre)*
1917 Publishes the novel *Abel Sánchez*
1920 Publishes the poem *The Christ of Velázquez (El Cristo de Velázquez)* and *Three Exemplary Novels and a Prologue (Tres novelas ejemplares y un prólogo)*
States candidacy for deputy but defeated in elections
Appointed vice rector of the University of Salamanca
1923 Publishes a book of poetry titled *Rhymes from Within (Rimas de dentro)*

1924 Publishes a book of poetry titled *Teresa*
Exiled to Fuerteventura in the Canary Islands because of a series of articles written against the king and later against the dictator, Primo de Rivera
Pardoned by Primo de Rivera, but rather than return to Spain, chooses voluntary exile in Paris
1925 Publishes the sonnets of exile, *From Fuerteventura to Paris (De Fuerteventura a París)*
Publishes the essay *The Agony of Christianity (La agonía del cristianismo)* in the French translation of Jean Cassou
1926 Writes the plays *Dream Shadows (Sombras de sueño)* and *The Other (El Otro)*
Publishes the autobiographical piece *How to Make a Novel (Cómo se hace una novela)* in the French translation of Jean Cassou
1927 Publishes the Spanish version of *How to Make a Novel*
1928 Publishes *Ballads of Exile (Romancero del destierro)*
1929 Writes the play *Brother John or The World Is a Stage (El hermano Juan o el mundo es teatro)*
1930 Returns to Spain after the fall of the dictatorship of Primo de Rivera
Continues to criticize the monarchy
1931 Elected deputy to the Constitutional Convention (Cortes Constituyentes)
Reinstated as rector of the University of Salamanca
Begins to criticize the Republican government
Publishes the Spanish version of *The Agony of Christianity*
1933 Publishes *St. Manuel Bueno, Martyr, and Three More Stories (San Manuel Bueno, mártir, y tres historias más)*
1934 Wife dies
Retires from the university and named lifetime rector, perpetual mayor of Salamanca, and first citizen of honor
Proposed as a candidate for the Nobel Prize for Literature
1936 Receives an honorary doctorate from Oxford
Relieved of lifetime rectorship by the Republican government

Restored to rectorship by Franco

Issues a message from the University of Salamanca to the universities and academies of the world informing them of the Spanish Civil War

Denounces fascism during the festivities of the *Día de la Hispanidad*

Relieved of rectorship by Franco

Confined to home by authorities

Dies suddenly December 31

1953   Denounced as the greatest Spanish heretic of modern times by Antonio de Pildáin y Zapiáin, Bishop of the Canary Islands

1957   *On the Tragic Sense of Life* and *The Agony of Christianity* placed on the *Index* by the Catholic Church

Sartre

1905   Born June 21 in Paris[1]

1906   Father dies

Taken to live in the home of maternal grandparents, Charles Schweitzer (uncle of Dr. Albert Schweitzer of Lambaréné) and Louise Guillemin

1916   Mother remarries a naval officer

1917   Goes with mother and stepfather to La Rochelle

1920   Returns to Paris to finish school

1929   Meets Simone de Beauvoir

Passes *agrégation*

Begins military service

1931   Leaves the military and becomes a teacher of philosophy in Le Havre

1933   Goes to the French Institute of Berlin to study philosophy and is influenced by the work of Husserl and Heidegger

1934   Writes the essay *The Transcendence of the Ego (La Transcendance de l'ego)*

1936   Publishes the essay *Imagination (L'Imagination)*, writes the story *Herostratus (Erostrate)*, and submits for publication the novel *Nausea (La Nausée)* under the title *Melancholia*

1937   Visits the Greek village of Enbrosio, which will become
       the setting for the play *The Flies (Les Mouches)*
1938   Writes *The Psyche (La Psyché)*, part of which will be
       incorporated into the essay *The Emotions: Outline of a
       Theory (Esquisse d'une théorie des émotions)*
       Publishes *Nausea*
1939   Publishes the story *The Wall (Le Mur)* and *The Emo-
       tions*
       Resumes military duty
       Begins work on the novel *The Age of Reason (L'Age de
       Raison)* and the philosophical treatise *Being and
       Nothingness: An Essay on Phenomenological Ontology
       (L'Etre et le Néant: Essai d'ontologie phénoménolo-
       gique)*
1940   Publishes the essay *The Psychology of Imagination
       (L'Imaginaire: Psychologie phénoménologique de l'imag-
       ination)*
       Captured by the Nazis and imprisoned
1941   Escapes from the Nazis   .
       Returns to teaching
       Joins Maurice Merleau-Ponty in founding a resistance
       group consisting of intellectuals
1943   Publishes *The Flies* and *Being and Nothingness*
       Meets Albert Camus
       Word "existentialism" introduced by Gabriel Marcel
1944   Meets Jean Genet
       Première of the play *No Exit (Huis-clos)*
1945   Publishes *No Exit* and the novels *The Age of Reason* and
       The Reprieve (Le Sursis), which will form the first two
       volumes of *Roads to Freedom (Les Chemins de la li-
       berté)*
       Goes to the United States as a correspondent for *Com-
       bat*, Camus' journal of the Resistance, and for *Le Figaro*
       Meets Roosevelt
       Publication of the first issue of *Les Temps Modernes*,
       the principal forum of the existentialist writers
       Delivers the lecture *Existentialism Is a Humanism
       (l'Existentialisme est un humanisme)*
1946   Publishes *Existentialism Is a Humanism*, the essay

Anti-Semite and Jew (Refléxions sur la question juive), and the plays *The Victors (Morts sans sépulture)*, *The Respectful Prostitute (La Putain respectueuse)*, and *The Chips Are Down (Les Jeux sont faits)*

1947　Publishes *Baudelaire* and begins publication of the essay *What Is Literature? (Qu'est-ce que la littérature?)* in *Les Temps Modernes*

Begins work on the *Morale*, which will not be published until after his death in 1983

1948　Publishes the plays *Dirty Hands (Les Mains sales)* and *In the Mesh (L'Engrenage)*

Joins the Revolutionary People's Assembly (R.D.R.)

Entire work placed on the *Index* by the Catholic Church

1949　Publishes the third volume of *Roads to Freedom*, titled *Troubled Sleep (La Mort dans l'âme)*

Officially resigns from the R.D.R.

1951　Writes the play *The Devil and the Good Lord (Le Diable et le bon Dieu)*

1952　Publishes the study of Jean Genet, titled *Saint Genet: Actor and Martyr (Saint Genet: Comédien et Martyr)*

Final break with Camus

Makes first visit to USSR.

1953　Première of the play *Kean*

1955　Brings out the play *Nekrassov*

Visits China with Simone de Beauvoir

1956　Makes plans with Roger Garaudy to compare existentialist and Marxist methods in a study of Flaubert

Meets Arlette El Kaïm, whom he will later adopt

1957　Publishes *Existentialism and Marxism (Existentialisme et Marxisme)*, which will later serve as the introduction to the philosophical treatise, *Critique of Dialectical Reason I: Theory of Practical Ensembles (Critique de la raison dialectique I: Théorie des ensembles pratiques)* and will be titled *Search for a Method (Questions de méthode)*

Protests the war in Algeria

1959　Completes the play *The Condemned of Altona (Les Sequéstrés d'Altona)*

1960　Publishes the *Critique of Dialectical Reason*

Visits Cuba with Simone de Beauvoir and meets Castro and Che Guevara

Visits Yugoslavia and meets Tito

1961 Continues the study of Flaubert

1963 Publishes the autobiographical piece *The Words (Les Mots)*

1964 Rejects the Nobel Prize for Literature

1965 Adopts Arlette El Kaïm

1966 Publishes sections of the study on Flaubert in *Les Temps Modernes*

Joins a tribunal investigating American war crimes in Vietnam

1969 Mother dies

1970 Expresses interest in Maoism

1971 Publishes the first two volumes of the study of Flaubert, titled *The Family Idiot (L'Idiot de la famille)*

1972 Publishes the third volume of *The Family Idiot*

1980 Dies April 14

1983 Publication of *Cahiers pour une morale*

1985 Publication of *Critique de la raison dialectique II: L'Intelligibilité de l'Histoire*

The Tragic Pursuit of Being

1. Life History

Biographical Perspective

Despite his death in 1980, Sartre continues to stand as a challenge to the fundamental social, political, moral, and philosophical structures of Western civilization. Though he faced many of the contradictions with which Unamuno struggled a generation earlier, he achieved in his work a synthesis unparalleled in modern culture. The key to his genius is to be found in his own words in *Saint Genet:* "Genius is not a gift but the way out that one invents in desperate cases."[1] It was in response to a certain desperate situation that his entire life's work was created. While biographical studies have attempted to identify this situation, its ultimate meaning is to be found in modern man's existential plight.

Sartre's personal and intellectual biography reflects not only the culture of France but certain elements of German origin. Raised in the home of his widowed mother, he was exposed to the Lutheranism of his German grandfather and the Catholicism of his French grandmother. The two grandparents, however, were indifferent to religion, and thus instilled in the young Sartre a kind of secular idealism. Later, Sartre would reveal that this idealism led him to literature and ultimately influenced his decision to become a writer.[2]

It was as an inspiring writer that Sartre chose to devote his university studies to philosophy. While preparing for the entrance examination for the Ecole Normale, he developed an interest in the essays of Bergson and came to believe that a

1

knowledge of philosophy would enable him to produce literary subjects of greater profundity. He regarded philosophy as a means to becoming a writer rather than as a discipline in which he might create a work of his own.

Though never a disciple of Bergson, Sartre discovered through the study of his work how consciousness could be made an object of philosophical inquiry. His interest in Bergson, however, quickly passed and as a student at the Ecole Normale he progressed to other philosophers, chief of whom was Descartes. After the completion of his university studies, the young Sartre proceeded to Berlin, where he enrolled in the French Institute. During this decisive period in his intellectual development, he undertook an intensive study of German phenomenology, concentrating on the work of Husserl and Heidegger. It was in response to the theories of Husserl that Sartre's own career as a philosopher began. In the mid-1930s he produced his first philosophical essay, *The Transcendence of the Ego*, in which he challenged certain fundamental premises of Husserl and phenomenology. Meanwhile, however, he chose to define himself as a phenomenologist, and though his thought would move through various stages during his lifetime, he would claim at the end that he had never ceased to think as a phenomenologist.[3]

In 1939 Sartre was called to join the French army at Nancy and from there was transferred to Alsace. He was soon captured by the Nazis and imprisoned. Though he escaped early the next year, the experience left a profound impression on him. The significance of this period in the life of Sartre has been clarified by Oreste Pucciani. He cites the *Mémoires* of Simone de Beauvoir.

> His optimism had not been destroyed by the events. This did not surprise me. . . . What did unsettle me was the rigidity of his moralism. . . . He surprised me in still another way. If he had come back to Paris, it was not to enjoy the comforts of his freedom, but to do something. . . . We had to break out of our isolation, unite, organize the resistance.[4]

Sartre's political commitment was thus born as a result of the war.

It is in this crucial experience that the origin of his theory of human relations is to be found. Pucciani argues that Sartre would come to interpret relationships in the private sphere in terms of the social conflict he witnessed during the war.[5] Though at the end of his life he would admit the possibility of a positive reciprocity between men,[6] the human relations described in his literary and philosophical works would remain fundamentally negative. It is for this reason that the war can be taken as the decisive influence on his adult life. It was a historic event experienced in the social sphere which stands in sharp contrast to the personal and ultimately religious crisis at the heart of Unamuno's work.

Though Sartre was involved in political activities throughout the 1940s, his great philosophical treatise of the period, *Being and Nothingness*, approached the human condition from the perspective of the individual. It was not until the 1950s that he placed his existential philosophy within an explicitly social framework and took on the problem of Marxism. Though he never joined the Party, he stated in the introduction to the *Critique* that Marxism was the unsurpassable philosophy of the twentieth century. Existentialism, on the other hand, was to be no more than an enclave within it. At first glance his comments suggested a complete revision of his earlier philosophical premises. A close reading of the *Critique*, however, revealed just the opposite of what he had announced in the introduction. Rather than subordinate existentialism to Marxism, he used existentialism to surpass the determinism that limited Marxism to the realm of nineteenth-century philosophy.

In his final work, *The Family Idiot*, Sartre synthesized the individual perspective of *Being and Nothingness* and the social theory of the *Critique*. With the instruments of his entire philosophical corpus in hand, he used the life of Flaubert to demonstrate the possibilities of existentialism as a method of inquiry. This was his definitive work and the culmination of his entire philosophical and literary enterprise.

Sartre's intellectual career represents, as he himself would repeat, an attempt to realize the ultimate consequences of a radical atheism. Unamuno, in contradistinction, would frequently return to religion in the hope of finding a salvation he held to be rationally impossible. The importance of religion in Unamuno's life began in early childhood. While Sartre was exposed to the secular idealism of his grandparents, Unamuno was raised in a strict Catholic environment. As a child he attended Mass daily and was a member of the Society of San Luis Gonzaga.

At the age of sixteen Unamuno left his native Bilbao to attend the University of Madrid. While there he discovered bourgeois positivism and socialism. Both influences quickly undermined the simple faith of his childhood. Soon he abandoned religious practices and concerned himself with strictly philosophical questions. He began to read Hegel in the original German and wrote a philosophical tract based on Hegelian thought which he titled *Logical Philosophy.* It was in the context of this early exposure to Hegel that Unamuno eventually concluded: "I believe that the foundation of my thought is Hegelian."[7]

It would be quite easy to consider these early Madrid years as an advancement from simple faith to mature reason. Such an interpretation, however, would be based on an assumption that the course of a human life evolves in a linear fashion. As Sartre has suggested in the introduction of the *Critique,* the pattern of a lifetime more closely resembles a spiral than a straight line. One returns again and again to the same experiences but at different levels of development and integration. It might be said that Unamuno did not complete the first orbit of his personal trajectory until 1897, when he suffered the most profound of his many religious crises. The young Hegelian of the 1880s had thus not destroyed the religious child of the 1860s and 1870s. He was simply the other face of what would become a complex and indeed troubled personality.

The religious crisis of 1897 was preceded by a period of intense political activity in the life of Unamuno. In 1894 he officially enrolled in the Bilbao branch of the Spanish Socialist Party and during the next several years contributed numerous articles to the socialist party organ, *La Lucha de Clases.*[8] Then, in 1896, his third son Raimundo was stricken with meningitis, developed hydrocephalus, and died. Unamuno would come to consider this the most tragic event in his life. He would even wonder if it was God's punishment for his own abandonment of the Catholic faith.

On a night in March of 1897 Unamuno left his home in Salamanca and went secretly to the Dominican monastery of San Esteban, where he remained for three days. He felt guilt over the loss of his childhood faith and prayed to recover it. He would later reveal, however, that what he wept "were tears of anguish, not repentance."[9] It was neither the death of his son nor, for that matter, the "death of God" in his life that elicited this response. Rather, it was the realization of his anguished desire for a fullness of being and the knowledge of his ultimate mortality.

The year 1897 is the pivotal period in Unamuno's personal and intellectual development. It represents the moment when the contradictions of his entire lifetime were reduced to a single cry of anguish. The great conflict of faith and reason—the heart says yes but the intellect says no—which most scholars see as the cornerstone of Unamuno's work, is lived in its most bitter intensity. Henceforth it will be possible to speak of an existentialist Unamuno.

After the crisis of 1897 Unamuno abandoned socialism and focused his attention on the problem of man's hunger for the absolute being which he lacks. It is for this reason that critics of the left would attack him as a kind of political turncoat. Unamuno, nevertheless, retained an interest in politics, and as Spain's leading intellectual of the day he exerted an important influence in the public sphere. In 1924 he wrote a series of articles against Alfonso XIII and the dictator, Miguel Primo de Rivera. As a result, he was exiled to Fuerteventura in the Canary Islands. Later in the year Primo de Rivera pardoned him, but Unamuno chose voluntary exile in Paris. He did not return to Spain until the death of Primo de Rivera in 1930. Once again on Spanish soil, he continued to attack the monarchy and was in part responsible for its downfall.

During the early 1930s Unamuno criticized the Republican government and was eventually relieved of his lifetime rectorship at the University of Salamanca for supposedly harboring fascist sympathies. In October of 1936, however, he responded to a speech of the fascist General Millán Astray and denounced fascism. As a result, he was confined to his home under virtual house arrest. Franco, in fact, gave the local authorities permission to execute him if they saw fit. Unamuno, however, died at the end of December, and for years the fascist government attempted to perpetuate the myth that he had somehow supported its anti-democratic activities. That Unamuno was not an ally of the traditional forces of Spanish reaction, however, is revealed by the fact that in 1953, the year of the Concordat between the Franco government and the Vatican, Unamuno was declared the greatest heretic of modern times.[10] In 1957 *On the Tragic Sense of Life* and *The Agony of Christianity* were placed on the Church's *Index* of forbidden books.

Autobiographical Perspective

While the biographies of Sartre and Unamuno reveal certain fundamental experiences which influenced their intellectual development, it is in the autobiographical pieces, *The Words* and *How to Make a Novel*, that we will discover the way in which they personally understood their lives. What they say about the fathers they both lost in early childhood is particularly revealing.

According to *The Words*, the death of Jean-Baptiste was the over-determining event of Sartre's childhood. He states in no uncertain terms that father-son relationships are negative to the extent that fathers confer an essence upon their sons and in so doing rob them of their freedom. It must be remembered, of course, that this stance was taken by Sartre not as a child but as a man of nearly sixty. It was Sartre's choice to view his fatherless childhood not merely as the result of contingency but as a kind of blessing. Whether he felt this as a child in the home of his grandparents in Paris or his stepfather in La Rochelle cannot be known. It is certain, however, that the situation had a tremendous impact on his future development.

Unamuno's attitude toward the father-figure is markedly different. Unlike Sartre, he knew his father and retained concrete memories of him. It would have been very peculiar, there-

6

fore, if he had taken the abstract, theoretical position of Sartre. As a child, Unamuno experienced a real dimension of human relations which Sartre never knew. Strangely enough, it was this contact with the real that in a certain sense would account for his faith in others and ultimately the idealism Sartre imputed to his thought.

In *How to Make a Novel* Unamuno reflects on his most vivid memory of his father. It happened that his father was speaking in a foreign language with someone in the drawing room of their home when Unamuno overheard them. To his surprise he was unable to understand a word of what they were saying. He stood bewildered and dumbfounded in the presence of a strange incantation that he would one day discover was French. This image of his father uttering incomprehensible words while, as he writes, secretly communicating with him across the room, was to remain with him for the rest of his life. It is an image of silent communion with the Other in the face of the alienating power of the spoken word. It is a memory of love which stands in sharp contrast to Sartre's empty memory of a man he never knew nor ever wished to meet.

The early childhood memories revealed in *The Words* and *How to Make a Novel* are not only of human relationships, either actual or imagined, but of words. Unamuno discovered the man behind the spoken word. Sartre, in the man's absence, turned to the written word of books. It was through books that he entered the world of ideas. "I found more reality in the idea," he states, "than in the thing because it was given to me first and because it was given as a thing."[11] Though seemingly straightforward, this statement reveals a certain problem. Why should it be a question of ideas or things? Is not the first contact a child has in the world with the Other? Sartre, it is clear, is attempting to explain the idealism of his youth. He turned to books as a child because there was no one to divert his attention. Though his father was dead, we are led to wonder where his mother and grandparents were when he made his first step into the world of idealism. Something remains unsaid in his recollections of childhood. It is the desperate situation he would come to see as the source of genius.

The Words and *How to Make a Novel* raise questions concerning not only the interconnectedness of human relationships and language, but God. Just as Sartre's real father was absent from his early life, so too was any belief in God the Father. Sartre relates how he was waiting one day for some schoolmates who were to accompany him to the *lycée*, when he decided to think about God. Suddenly, he writes, God tumbled from the heavens and disappeared into thin air. Never again would Sartre assume a belief in God. This, however, was not the end of the matter, for although God the Father had been laid to rest, the Holy Spirit was to remain with him for some time. It was a hidden and misunderstood belief in the Holy Spirit, he writes, that lay at the heart of his early idealism. The Holy Spirit was the Other that Sartre never knew. He had come to haunt him through an illusion created by lonely children and all those who aspire to be creators.

It is in terms of the Holy Spirit that Unamuno resolves the questions raised in *How to Make a Novel*. The voice of the absolute Other for Unamuno is not that of God but of society. It is not a promise of fulfillment but a threat. Freedom abhors the word that catches it from behind and enchains it. Yet freedom discovers what the child Unamuno always knew—that behind the spoken word is a silent word, that behind alienation lies communion, that the anguish of nothingness is but a moment of a more profound ontological structure that in philosophy is called the *Mitsein*[12] but for Unamuno is simply brotherly love. It is here that Unamuno hears the voice of the Holy Spirit in whom he was rationally unable to believe.

In the autobiographical pieces we discover the original choice of Sartre and Unamuno to become writers. They make surprisingly similar statements on the matter. "The eagerness to write," Sartre tells us, "involves a refusal to live."[13] "Literature," in the words of Unamuno, "is nothing but death."[14] Such negativity is indeed strange from men who would eventually be regarded as the most significant writers of twentieth-century France and Spain.

It is Sartre's contention that the writer denies life to the extent that he chooses the imaginary over the real in the vain and absurd hope of endowing being with necessity and thereby saving man from contingency. The desire to write is born on the ruins of religion. It involves the same belief that haunted his own early years and could be purged only through the arduous project of atheism. In the end Sartre would come to see the enterprise of the writer as ill-advised and misguided. He would compare his disillusion with literature to that of Swann with Odette: " 'To think that I messed up my life for a woman who wasn't my type!' "[15]

While Sartre would claim to have made the wrong choice, Unamuno would take writing as his destiny. For Unamuno writing is not one of many activities; it represents life itself. The writer takes pen in hand in the hope of endowing himself with the absolute being which he lacks. As the words appear on the paper, however, he loses himself in his creation. This, Unamuno would hold, is the profound meaning of the metaphor of the spirit become flesh. It is not the fulfillment of eternal desire but its absolute degradation and ultimately its death. Unamuno would hope to achieve a sort of communion with his fellow man through writing but in the end all that remained would be a book. It could not be otherwise. It was his fate and the fate of all who attempt to inscribe themselves in what he would call the novel of life.

2. Philosophy

The Philosophy of Sartre

The key to Sartre's entire philosophical enterprise is freedom. Freedom is man's ultimate goal, yet the attainment of freedom is possible only because man is fundamentally free. Action both requires and affirms the freedom of the individual performing the action. It is in this context that philosophical inquiry itself can be said to possess a moral dimension. Sartre stated in 1946 that the man who seeks is already ethical.[1] To a society which takes man as a means rather than an end, such a radical position on the "truth of freedom" might seem politically dangerous. In the world of the computer it becomes somewhat irrelevant. Nonetheless, it is as a philosopher of freedom that Sartre stands at a crossroads today. Will he be, as certain intellectuals proclaim, the "last philosopher" or will the dialogue continue? Will freedom be no more than a time-worn cliché of the capitalist societies or will it remain "the absolute at the heart of relativity itself"?[2]

The philosophical writings of Sartre can be divided into five general periods: (1) The early essays; (2) *Being and Nothingness*; (3) *Saint Genet*; (4) The *Critique of Dialectical Reason*; and (5) *The Family Idiot*. Of the first period the most important essays are *The Transcendence of the Ego* and *The Psychology of Imagination*. The works of the second and fourth periods are strictly philosophical while those of the third and fifth are "biographies" that combine philosophy, psychology, social theory, and literature. It is in the early essays,

Being and Nothingness, and the *Critique* that we find the instruments that will enable us to elucidate the unwritten philosophy of Unamuno and to discover the meaning behind his literature. These works are the key to our entire enterprise.

The Early Essays

In *The Transcendence of the Ego* Sartre accepts the theory of Husserl that consciousness is always and only "consciousness of something." In a way similar to Ortega y Gasset, however, he challenges Husserl's theory of the phenomenological reduction.[3] He argues that consciousness cannot be studied in isolation but only in and through its relation to the object of which it is conscious. In itself, consciousness is a pure intentionality which, through the positing of an object, continually transcends itself. It is in its object, therefore, rather than in itself, that a unity of consciousness is to be found.

Sartre further distinguishes between pre-reflective and reflective consciousness. Pre-reflective consciousness is a positional consciousness of an object but a non-positional consciousness of itself. Nevertheless, while pre-reflective consciousness makes no attempt to posit itself as an object, a "self-consciousness" (*conscience* [*de*] *soi*) does exist.[4] In other words, consciousness is "conscious" of being conscious of its object.

In contrast to pre-reflective consciousness, reflective consciousness attempts to posit itself as an object. It is on this level of consciousness, therefore, that we find the Cartesian *cogito.* Reflective consciousness, however, never succeeds in apprehending itself as a veritable object nor in achieving what Sartre calls a "reflective scissiparity." If it did so, it would cease to be consciousness.

Though consciousness does not transform itself into an object, the process of reflection results in the creation of the Ego (psyche). Specifically, the Ego as "I" is the ideal unity of all the actions of consciousness while the Ego as "Me" is the ideal unity of all the states of consciousness. The Ego, therefore, is not consciousness itself but an objectification of consciousness. It is an object in the world, knowable both to the consciousness which constitutes it and to other consciousnesses.

11

While the Ego is personal, consciousness is pre-personal. This does not mean, however, that all consciousnesses are the same, since each differs precisely in egological structure and according to historical, social, and cultural conditions. It simply means that consciousness is not the psyche but rather the pure spontaneity that lies at the heart of human reality. This radical theory of consciousness, first formulated in *The Transcendence of the Ego*, would gain full expression in *Being and Nothingness* and would make possible the existential psychoanalyses of Genet and Flaubert.

In *The Psychology of Imagination* Sartre outlines a theory of imagination that would lead to an understanding of the nothingness of consciousness and its ultimate freedom. He argues that an "imagining" consciousness differs from a "realizing" consciousness insofar as it posits its object as nonexistent. The act of imagining thus involves a simultaneous affirmation of the unreal and negation of the real. This ability of consciousness to negate the real means that in its relation to the real it is free.

> We can affirm fearlessly that if consciousness is a succession of determined psychical facts, it is entirely impossible for it ever to produce anything but the real. For a consciousness to be able to imagine it must be able to escape from the world by its very nature, it must be able by its own efforts to withdraw from the world. In a word it must be free.[5]

It is as a negation of the real that Sartre approaches the problem of art. The real, he states, is completely contingent and for this reason never beautiful. "Beauty is a value applicable only to the imaginary and which means the negation of the world in its essential structure."[6] The artist flees the contingency of reality and seeks necessity in his work. His effort, however, is in vain and in the end he succeeds only in turning man back upon his own nothingness.

In *What Is Literature?* Sartre would explain how the "committed" artist can bring man to a heightened awareness of his freedom and engage him in purposeful action in the world. Nevertheless, the fundamental premise of *The Psychol-*

ogy of the Imagination would remain intact and would be developed in *The Family Idiot* into a final theory of art. In this theory the long history of Western aesthetics, born in the marketplaces of Athens, would find both its culmination and undoing.

Being and Nothingness

It is in *Being and Nothingness* that Sartre fully elucidates the problems introduced in *The Transcendence of the Ego* and *The Psychology of Imagination* and formulates his ontology. He begins with a discussion of the relationship between consciousness and the being of which it is conscious. "Consciousness is consciousness *of* something. This means that transcendence is the constitutive structure of consciousness; that is, that consciousness is born *supported by* a being which is not itself. This is what we call the ontological proof."[7] Consciousness, in its being, is a revelation of being. For this reason, being logically precedes the consciousness of being. "To say that consciousness is consciousness of something is to say that it must produce itself as a revealed-revelation of a being which is not it and which gives itself as already existing when consciousness reveals it" (p. lxii).

This logical priority of being over consciousness permits Sartre to respond to the argument of Berkeley that *"esse est percipi"* ("being is being perceived"). Sartre holds that while being is completely present in a particular phenomenon, the phenomenon appears to consciousness on the foundation of being. He calls this the transphenomenality of being and states: "The being of that which *appears* does not exist *only* in so far as it appears" (p. lxii). Were the being of the phenomenon reducible to the phenomenon of being, then consciousness by itself could found being. *Esse* would be *percipi*. Being, however, is absolutely contingent. It surpasses the consciousness of being and is the condition of all knowledge of being.

Sartre calls the being of which consciousness is conscious "being-in-itself" *(être-en-soi)*. This In-itself[8] "is" what it is and contains no negation. It is absolute plenitude.

Nevertheless, Sartre asks how it is possible to conceive of a negative judgment if there is only a fullness of being. His reply is that there exists a non-being which is the contradictory of the In-itself. He calls this non-being "being-for-itself" *(être-pour-soi)*. The domain of the For-itself is consciousness. Consciousness is a non-being because it can be described only through its relationship to a being which it is not. It is, moreover, an "internal negation" of being. This means that it negates the In-itself through a process whereby it realizes itself as consciousness of not being the In-itself.

Though the In-itself is "everything" and the For-itself "nothing," the For-itself is what Sartre calls the great adventure of being. The In-itself does not depend on the For-itself, but without the For-itself there would appear no objects as such. Through the negation of the For-itself, the In-itself comes to be differentiated. The meaning of being thus arises through the For-itself. Meaning is not something that resides in being. Instead, it is the For-itself as a relation to the In-itself.

Despite the internal negation of the For-itself, the In-itself remains unaffected in its being. "It is enough to say that the original phenomenon of knowledge *adds* nothing to being and creates nothing. It does not enrich being, for knowledge is pure negativity" (p. 179). Knowledge, it might be said, is simply the manner in which the In-itself is revealed as not being the For-itself. It is, however, not only a negation of being but a simultaneous affirmation. Because of knowledge, being becomes a "being-there." "The For-itself by its self-negation becomes the affirmation of the In-itself." (p. 217) Thus, through absolute nothingness the great silence of being is broken.

If the For-itself can be called the adventure of being, this is because in its being it is free. Sartre states: "This possibility which human reality has to secrete a nothingness . . . is *freedom*" (pp. 24–25). In other words, the For-itself is free precisely because it is nothing. Though bound to being in a relationship which Sartre calls the "facticity of freedom,"[9] it precedes any essence or meaning which might come to qualify it.

Human freedom precedes essence in man and makes it possible; the essence of the human being is suspended in his freedom. What we call freedom is impossible to distinguish from the *being* of "human reality." Man does not exist *first* in order to be free

14

subsequently; there is no difference between the being of man
and his *being-free.* (p. 25)

Freedom is neither a "right" nor a "privilege," as the capitalist
democracies maintain, but the very being which is man.

The facticity of freedom is ultimately a temporal rather
than a spatial relation to being. As a "presence" to being, it is a
rejection of past being and a projection toward future being.
While for Einstein time is to be found in things, Sartre asserts
that it is the relationship of consciousness to things. This
means, however, that man can know only "human" time.

Sartre clarifies the ontological structure of the Ego in
terms of time. The Ego is the past being to which consciousness is present. Sartre refers to Hegel's famous statement, *"Wesen ist was gewesen ist"* ("Being is what has been")
(p. 35), to argue that the Ego, which is the "has been" of consciousness, is its essence. It is precisely because consciousness
is forever separated from its essence by nothingness that it
experiences itself in anguish. "This *self* with its *a priori* and
historical content is the *essence* of man. Anguish as the manifestation of freedom in the face of the self means that man is
always separated by a nothingness from his essence" (p. 35).

The concept of anguish is fundamental to an understanding of existentialism. In addition to boredom and nausea, anguish is what Sartre calls a "revealing intuition" of being. It is
the "mode of being of freedom as consciousness of being; it is
in anguish that freedom is, in its being, in question for itself"
(p. 29).

Sartre uses the term *ekstasis,* in the Greek sense of a
"standing-out-from," to describe further the relation of consciousness to the being of which it is conscious. There are, he
argues, three successive *ekstases.* The first is the temporal
ekstasis, in which consciousness, as presence to being, exists as
the internal negation of being. The second, introduced in *The
Transcendence of the Ego,* is reflection. In what Sartre calls the
"circuit of ipseity" consciousness, after spontaneously realizing that it is not its object, turns inward in an effort to posit
itself as an object and endow itself with the being which it
lacks. This endeavor, however, is doomed to failure, for were

15

consciousness to become an object, it would cease to be consciousness. This would be its death.

Sartre proceeds to differentiate good faith from bad faith in terms of the reflective *ekstasis*. While good faith is the attempt of consciousness to escape its anguish by turning to the In-itself, bad faith arises when consciousness turns to itself which it envisions as In-itself. It strives to take itself not as it is, that is, as a freedom, but as the self it is not, namely as a thing. Both good faith and bad faith are vain attempts to escape oneself, but bad faith denies the failure. The man of bad faith lives in what Sartre, based on his reading of Nietzsche, calls the "spirit of seriousness." Sartre defines the spirit of seriousness in the following terms.

> It is obvious that the serious man at bottom is hiding from himself the consciousness of his freedom; he is in *bad faith* and his bad faith aims at presenting himself to his own eyes as a consequence; everything is a consequence for him, and there is never any beginning. That is why he is so concerned with the consequences of his acts. Marx proposed the original dogma of the serious when he asserted the priority of object over subject. Man is serious when he takes himself for an object. (p. 580)

While consciousness is unable to achieve a veritable objectivity through reflection, it discovers in the third *ekstasis* that it does possess a degree of objectivity in the eyes of the Other. Sartre calls this third *ekstasis* "being-for-others" (*être-pour-autrui*). The For-others, however, does not represent a third mode of being, and Sartre states: "Our human reality must of necessity be simultaneously for-itself and for-others" (p. 282).

The For-itself discovers the For-others when it is made an object of the Other's look. It is shame (or pride) that reveals this look to the For-itself. Shame is fundamentally the For-itself's recognition of its objectivity. Through the Other, the interiority of the For-itself is given an exterior dimension.

Through the For-others, Sartre further develops the theory of the psyche introduced in *The Transcendence of the Ego*. The For-others is an object in the world and as such is comparable to the "Me" of the Ego. Sartre contends, however, that the look

16

is experienced at the very heart of consciousness and that as a result, a self comes to "haunt" pre-reflective consciousness.

The Other is not given to consciousness as an object, for were that the case, there would be no meaning to his look. Rather, he is given directly as a For-itself. The Other must be a freedom because through his look, consciousness experiences itself as a kind of object. It is in "self-defense" that consciousness thus objectifies the Other. By making the Other a "being-for-me," consciousness attempts to free itself from its "being-for-the-other." Following this reasoning, Sartre comes to a shocking conclusion: "The essence of the relations between consciousnesses is not the *Mitsein;* it is conflict" (p. 429).

Sartre describes the For-others as a fall toward objectivity but holds that if this objectivity were ever reached, consciousness would cease to be consciousness. Consciousness never "knows" itself as an object and the For-others is ultimately an experience of malaise. "My being for-others is a fall through absolute emptiness toward objectivity. . . . Thus myself-as-object is neither knowledge nor a unity of knowledge but an uneasiness, a lived wrenching away from the ekstatic unity of the for-itself, a limit which I can not reach and which yet I am" (pp. 274–75).

For Sartre there is no *Mitsein* and the "We/Us" is never constituted ontologically. The "Us-Object," which is revealed through the look of a third,[10] and the "We-Subject," which is revealed to a particular consciousness through the world of manufactured objects,[11] involve no deep reciprocity. The "We/Us" is in fact always experienced by an individual consciousness. The For-others thus precedes any "With-others," and the latter would be simply a more complex form of the former.

It is in terms of the For-others that Sartre describes language. Language, he argues, arises as a being-for-others. Like knowledge, it is not itself a being but rather a relationship between two beings. On the most fundamental level, man is language to the extent that he exists in an ontological relation with the Other. "Language is not a phenomenon added on to

17

being-for-others. It *is* originally being-for-others; that is, it is the fact that a subjectivity experiences itself as an object for the Other" (p. 372).

Despite the objectivity which consciousness experiences in the presence of the Other, it remains, in the final analysis, a non-being. As such, however, it is not only a lack of being but a desire for being. It is in terms of this ontological desire that Sartre undertakes an analysis of God. Consciousness, he states, desires to be Supreme Being. He defines this ultimate but impossible goal of consciousness as the foundation of the In-it-self-For-itself or, in the words of the Scholastics, the *ens-causa-sui.*

The key to the In-itself-For-itself is to be found in the terms "possibility" and "value." The possible, Sartre argues, is that which the For-itself must attain in order to be. It is a specific thing and relates to a concrete action in the world. "What is given as the *peculiar lack* of each for-itself and what is defined as lacking to precisely this for-itself and no other is the possibility of the for-itself" (p. 96). In contrast to the possible, value is beyond all transcendence. It might be called the "In-itself" of consciousness. "The for-itself is defined ontologically as a *lack of being,* and possibility belongs to the for-itself as that which it lacks, in the same way that value haunts the for-itself as the totality of being which is lacking" (p. 565).

While the For-itself desires the being which it lacks, it desires it as itself.

> Human reality is the desire of being-in-itself. But the in-itself which it desires can not be pure contingent, absurd in-itself, comparable at every point to that which it encounters and which it nihilates. . . . It is as consciousness that it wishes to have the impermeability and infinite density of the in-itself. It is as the nihilation of the in-itself and a perpetual evasion of contingency and of facticity that it wishes to be its own foundation. This is why the possible is projected in general as what the for-itself lacks in order to become in-itself-for-itself. The fundamental value which presides over this project is exactly the in-itself-for-itself; that is, the ideal of a consciousness which would be the foundation of its own being-in-itself by the pure consciousness which it would have of itself. It is this ideal which can be called

God. Thus the best way to conceive of the fundamental project of human reality is to say that man is the being whose project is to be God. (pp. 565–66)

This project of becoming God in a sense defines man and comes close to endowing him with an essence. It is, however, never constituted as such, and man remains nothing but desire. "Everything happens," Sartre concludes, "as if the world, man, and man-in-the-world succeeded in realizing only a missing God" (p. 623).

For Sartre the concept of God is contradictory precisely because the For-itself and the In-itself are by definition contradictory modes of being. Since man is given as a desire for an impossible synthesis of these two modes of being, he might be called tragic. Sartre, however, chooses to end *Being and Nothingness* by calling him a "useless passion."

Critique of Dialectical Reason

In the *Critique of Dialectical Reason*, Sartre takes the ontology of *Being and Nothingness* and uses it to create a theory of history. In order to accomplish this task he realizes the need for a new method of inquiry. In the introduction to the *Critique*, titled *Search for a Method*, he outlines a methodology which combines both analysis and synthesis. He calls it the "regressive-progressive" method. The regressive-progressive method is "dialectical reason." It is a method that will not only make possible the elucidation of the fundamental project of historical man but will make history intelligible. When carried to its limits, he claims, it will reveal the "truth of history."

The first volume of the *Critique* is a regressive-analytical study that deconstructs history and attempts to explain its various structures, chief of which are the practico-inert, the series, the group-in-fusion, the institution, the sovereign, and social classes. The recently published second volume was intended to be a progressive-synthetic study which, through the example of the Soviet Union, would reconstruct history. The work, however, was never completed.[12] It would be Sartre's decision to study the individual history of Flaubert in preference to a collective history. It is in *The Family Idiot*, therefore,

19

rather than the *Critique*, that the full implications of the regressive-progressive method are drawn.

In the first volume of the *Critique*[13] Sartre treats the problem of dialectics and the relation of Marxism to existentialism. He begins by studying the "materialistic" dialectic of later generations of Marxists. He states that this dialectic is in fact "idealistic" as knowledge of it is beyond the scope of any individual investigator. It would be what he calls an "exterior" dialectic, existing in nature and in man only insofar as he is a part of nature. In principle, consciousness would be unable to understand fully its structures. This, in turn, would mean that history, in the final analysis, is unknowable.

Sartre agrees that a dialectic of nature might exist but adds that at the present moment in history its structures can only by hypothesized. He chooses, therefore, to study the dialectic where he finds it: in the context of human reality. In place of a materialist dialectic he offers a "realist" dialectic which operates between two sectors of materiality: praxis and things.[14] This realist dialectic, he argues, will make possible a knowledge of history.

Sartre defines the dialectic in terms of a totalization. While a totality can exist only as the correlative of an imagining consciousness, a totalization is action in development. He states that from an ontological point of view, the dialectic is a totalization, while in terms of epistemology, it is the accessibility of totalization to a knowledge which is itself totalizing. Dialectical reason might thus be described as a "reflexive retotalization."

Sartre contrasts dialectical reason with analytical reason and places the problem of rationalities in its historical context. It is his contention that analytical reason breaks a whole into parts while dialectical reason provides for a synthesis of parts into a whole. Analytical reason, therefore, is a moment of dialectical reason. In the nineteenth century, however, bourgeois positivism ignored the synthetic moment of the thought process, not only because analysis was its weapon against the myths of throne and altar but because analysis atomized the individuals of society and prevented the proletariat from advancing to the level of class-consciousness. Marxism, as we know it, surpassed this bourgeois negativity yet failed to account for the individual moment that makes a synthetic whole, or a class, intelligible. It is because Sartre reinstates the individual within the collective that the *Critique* has been interpreted by many as a "corrected" Marxism.

In contrast to *Being and Nothingness*, the *Critique* presents man in terms not only of desire but of need. "Everything is to be explained through *need (le besoin)*; need is the first totalising relation between the material being, man, and the material ensemble of which he is a part. This relation is *univocal*, and *of interiority*."[15]

The man of need is simultaneously a man of labor. Sartre states that need is praxis and that human labor is "the original *praxis* by which man produces and reproduces his life" (p. 90). While in *Being and Nothingness* consciousness discovered itself in and through the object of which it was conscious, in the *Critique* need discovers itself in and through the object on which it labors. In labor, moreover, man makes himself into a tool in order to satisfy himself as need. There is, then, a kind of reification of man which precedes any contact with others.

As in *Being and Nothingness* the appearance of the Other is man's downfall. Through the presence of the Other, man discovers the great law of the world to which all are subject: scarcity. Scarcity manifests itself to men of need laboring in the same practical field. Sartre defines it as a "fundamental relation of *our* History and a contingent determination of our univocal relation to materiality" (p. 125). Scarcity, it might be said, simply means that there is not enough in the environment to satisfy everyone's need.

It is because of scarcity that there is violence. "The origin of struggle always lies, in fact, in some concrete antagonism whose material condition is *scarcity (la rareté)*, in a particular form, and the real aim is objective conquest or even creation, in relation to which the destruction of the adversary is the only means" (p. 113). This definition of human conflict alters the theory of being-for-others expounded in *Being and Nothingness*. Here, matter is the fundamental mediation between men, and it is only in reference to matter that the ontological threat posed by the Other has meaning.

21

The goal of the Other is to destroy "me" as a freedom so that he may obtain the object which "we" both need in order to survive. "My" violence, therefore, arises as counter-violence. The Other, in this context, is seen as absolute evil and must be annihilated at any cost.

> I may try to kill, to torture, to enslave, or simply to mystify, but in any case my aim will be to eliminate alien freedom as a hostile force, a force which can expel me from the practical field and make me into "a surplus man" condemned to death. In other words, it is undeniable that what I attack is man as man, that is, as the free *praxis* of an organic being. It is man, and nothing else, that I hate in the enemy, that is, in myself as Other; and it is myself that I try to destroy in him, so as to prevent him destroying me in my own body. (p. 133)

It is in the *Critique* that Sartre comes to define matter in terms of the practico-inert. He argues that man never knows pure matter: "If he could encounter pure matter in experience, he would have to be either a god or a stone" (pp. 181–82). Matter in fact always appears as worked matter. The practico-inert is thus what Sartre calls an "immaterial matter." It can be defined specifically as things insofar as they are mediated by man and man insofar as he is mediated by things. Sartre states: "At any moment of History things are human precisely to the extent that men are things" (p. 180). If the practico-inert exists, however, it is because of man: "Man is precisely the material reality from which matter gets its human functions" (p. 182). It is praxis, then, when inscribed in things, that turns back against praxis and reifies it.

A clear example of a practico-inert being is language. While in *Being and Nothingness* Sartre grounded language *(langage)* in being-for-others, in the *Critique* he grounds language *(langue)* in matter. Words, he states, are matter which has been mediated by man. They carry the projects of the Other into me and my projects into the Other. He continues: "Words live off the death of men, they come together through men; whenever I form a sentence its meaning escapes from me, is stolen from me; meanings are changed *for everyone* by each speaker and each day; the meanings of the very words in my mouth are changed by others" (p. 98). Language is thus an immaterial matter through which praxis experiences both unity and alterity.

It is in terms of the practico-inert that Sartre describes the inertia of praxis. Praxis is inert when the praxis that has been inscribed in things works through it. This is the meaning of passivity. It is a structure that profoundly alters the course of human history.

Man is born into a world of humanized materialities and discovers at a certain age a future prescribed for him in things. In the case of the worker, determinism is to be found in the machine. The machine is a worked object which contains the past praxis of the capitalist. Through it, the worker is made into a thing. It is in this context that Sartre is able to arrive at a definition of class-being.

> Class-being, as practico-inert being mediated by the passive syntheses of worked matter, comes to men through men; for each of us it is our being-outside-ourselves in matter and, in so far as this produces us and awaits us from birth, in so far as it constitutes itself through us as a future-fatality, that is to say as a future which will necessarily realise itself through us, through the otherwise arbitrary actions which we choose. (pp. 238–39)

Class-being is characterized by "interest" and "destiny." Both refer to a certain relationship between man and thing in a social field. The thing is man's interest if in this relationship he is an active subject; it is his destiny if he is a passive subject. The machine is thus the capitalist's interest and the worker's destiny.

When individuals recognize their common interest/destiny, they achieve a kind of identity. This identity, however, is alienating since through it each is the same as the Other to the extent that he is other than himself. It represents a unity in alterity which Sartre calls "seriality." In seriality "the Other is me in every Other and every Other in me and everyone as Other in all the Others" (pp. 266–67). Sartre identifies seriality in a wide array of human activities ranging from mass-consumerism to patriotism to racism.

Serialized man is the object of what Sartre, based on his

reading of American sociology, calls "other-direction" *(extéro-conditionnement).* Man is "other-directed" when a special interest group (whether Nazi anti-Semites or Madison Avenue advertisers) manipulate his serial relations in order to achieve certain ends. Other-directed man acts as every other man in the hope of being the same. In the process, however, he destroys any possibility of direct reciprocity with the Other.

Direct reciprocity between men is possible only when they attempt to negate their serial relations. What Sartre calls the "group-in-fusion" represents the moment when men are no longer unified in alterity but in their joint effort to transcend alterity. Such a group forms in a moment of common danger and marks the beginning of revolution.

The group-in-fusion is not an object but rather the common structure of each individual's action. It is in a sense a collective praxis. In this group "my" fellow-man is no longer other than "me" but the same. He is the lived objectivity of "my" subjectivity. Though the group-in-fusion makes possible a positive reciprocity among men, it nevertheless arises in a world of scarcity where human relations remain antagonistic. In order to survive, it must struggle with opposing groups which aim to destroy it. In the process it takes on the practico-inert structures it hoped to dissolve. It becomes an institution and its leader a sovereign. Because of scarcity, revolution thus fails. Man is condemned to alienation, and only in an ever-distant future will he be able to realize his project of freedom.

Despite such oppressive determinism, man remains the maker of history. This is because man in his being is free. There is thus a truth of history which might be called the truth of freedom. It is a "truth in becoming." In the *Critique* Sartre simply articulates this truth to itself and brings it to the level of reflexivity.

Toward a Philosophy of Unamuno

While Unamuno never produced a philosophical treatise comparable to *Being and Nothingness* or the *Critique of Dialectical Reason,* he believed that his work contained the intuitions that might one day be elucidated and developed into a philosophical system. He stated that his approach to readers

24

was Socratic,[16] and that rather than impose upon them a rigid philosophical system, he hoped to stimulate them to formulate thoughts of their own. "My endeavor has been, still is and will always be to make those who read me think and meditate on fundamentals. I have always sought to agitate and, at most, to suggest rather than instruct. If I start to sell bread, it will not be bread, but yeast and leavening."[17]

Unamuno is a champion of human freedom. In contrast to Sartre, however, he contends that philosophy, as constituted knowledge, is not only unable to express freedom but in a sense comes to inhibit it. In the term "philosophy of freedom" he would find a logical contradiction at the heart of which lies an ethical problem. Is it "right" for a philosopher of freedom to systematize his thought? His answer would be no.

> I have friends, good friends, who advise me to leave off this labor and to retire to construct what they call an objective work, "something definitive," they say, "something constructive, something lasting." They mean something dogmatic. I declare myself incapable of such a task and I demand my liberty, my holy liberty, even to the point of being able to contradict myself, if necessary. . . . To agitate is after all something. If, thanks to this agitation, another man follows and constructs something lasting, my work will last in his.[18]

While Sartre is not this "other" of whom Unamuno speaks, the instruments provided by his philosophical system will permit us to discover and in a sense to "create" the existentialist philosophy that Unamuno chose not to write. In so doing we will not undermine his fundamental intuition of freedom but rather make it accessible to others. In the process we will gain a more profound understanding of the structures that enchain freedom and ultimately of the means by which freedom might emancipate itself.

Being and Nothingness

Unamuno the "philosopher" is first of all an ontologist. It is in terms of ontology that he discusses the problems of human relations, knowledge, language, imagination, and God. As an ontologist his point of departure is contingency. "Existence has no reason for being because it is beyond all reasons. Those who found the reason of existence in a Being which is supreme, absolute, infinite, and eternal move in a *petitio principii*, in an enormous, vicious circle."[19] For Unamuno as well as Sartre, being precedes the meaning of being. It is this that permits us to call him an existentialist.

While Sartre gives priority to being over nothingness, Unamuno's ontology begins and ends in nothingness. This nothingness is to be found not only in the realm of human beings but in things. In *The Agony of Christianity* Unamuno reiterates the words of Père Hyacinthe: "I have a sort of instinctive perception of the nothingness of being, the nothingness of things, the nothingness of people."[20]

Although nothingness exists in things, it is man who discovers it within himself. "As one delves within oneself, the deeper one goes the more one discovers one's inanity, the truth that one is not altogether oneself, not what one wants to be, and, in short, that one is nothing."[21] This personal knowledge of nothingness produces what Unamuno calls a "hunger for being." However, because nothingness is man's nature, the hunger can never be satisfied. For this reason Unamuno calls him a diseased being. "Man, because he is man, because he possesses consciousness, is already, in comparison to the jackass or the crab, a sick animal. Consciousness is a disease."[22]

The intuition of consciousness as nothing but an insatiable hunger for a being which it is not, is what Unamuno calls the "tragic sense of life." It is an experience of anguish *(congoja)*[23] and it is the point of departure for any discussion of man or for any knowledge which man might have about himself.

> There is something which, for want of a better name, we shall call the tragic sense of life, and it carries along with it an entire conception of the Universe and of life itself, an entire philosophy more or less formulated, more or less conscious. . . . And this sense does not so much flow from ideas as determine them, even if though later these ideas react upon it and corroborate it.[24]

It is in terms of this tragic sense that Unamuno's entire concept of human reality will be cast.

26

While Sartre defines nothingness as the contradictory of being, for Unamuno it is simply an absence of being. According to certain critics this absence is in fact something. François Meyer, for example, states that nothing in Unamuno is something, but "a something which, opposite the all, the infinite, is *like nothing*."[25] If this were the case, then Unamuno could be taken as a Christian thinker and his thought compared with that of Pascal: "Because in fact what is man in nature? A nothingness in regard to the infinite, an all in regard to nothingness, a medium between nothing and everything."[26] Unamuno's conception of nothingness, however, is more radical than that permitted by Christian philosophy, and in an illuminating passage of his unpublished diary he reveals: "I have no soul, no spiritual substance; I have only states of consciousness which will vanish with the body which sustains them."[27]

Unamuno denies the existence of a soul and through the tragic sense reveals an intuition of the nothingness of consciousness which Sartre would theorize in *Being and Nothingness*. Nevertheless, when he speaks of a nothingness of things, he enters a realm of ontology not touched by Sartre.

In his early writings Unamuno speaks not of a nothingness of things but an inner being which is eternal and absolute. As his thought evolves, however, he rejects any noumenal reality and in *How to Make a Novel* replaces it with nothingness. He speaks metaphorically of a Japanese lacquered box. ". . . one of those lacquered Japanese boxes which contains another box, and that box still another, and that one still another again, each one carved and decorated according to the artist's ability, and then one final, tiny box—empty."[28] What was once the substance of things disappears and all that remains is appearance: "There are no interiors, the exterior is impermeable and things are as they seem."[29] With his own particular humor, Unamuno concludes in phenomenological terms: "The noumenon invented by Kant is about the most 'phenomenal' possible and . . . substance is what is most formal. The essence of a thing is its surface."[30]

Though Unamuno describes a kind of monism of phenomena, his conception of nothingness precludes a theory of what

Sartre calls the transphenomenality of being. In a sense he sees the phenomenon as an object hanging in mid-air. It is in this context that Meyer states: "Things are but appearance and dream, a pure phenomenal apparition without support: they float by themselves over a bottomless void."[31] Thus, it might paradoxically be said that the only "in-itself" being in Unamuno's thought is nothingness itself.

Through his rejection of the noumenon, nevertheless, Unamuno departs from the tradition of Spanish essentialism which distinguishes between an inner being *(ser)* and an outer being *(parecer)*. He avoids the dualism suggested by the two Spanish verbs "to be" (*ser* and *estar*) and ultimately what Sartre, in the words of Nietzsche, condemned in traditional philosophy: "the illusion of worlds-behind-the-scene."[32]

Being-for-Others

Although man in Unamuno is characterized by a profound nothingness, he possesses an objective being called *"serse."*[33] *"Serse,"* he states, "is being-for-itself, and being-for-itself is being-for-others."[34] He clarifies this in an illuminating passage. "He who is not in himself others and for-others, he who lacks representation, is not himself, is not for-himself, lacks personality. . . . Who is oneself? The one who represents, the one who is for-others."[35] In contrast to the "For-itself-For-others" of Sartre, the *serse* is more suggestive of the psyche. It possesses both subjective and objective dimensions. It might be said that the terms "for-itself" and "for-others" of Unamuno correspond to the terms "I" and "Me" of Sartre. The *serse*, nevertheless, is unique to Unamuno and can be taken as his most important contribution to existential ontology.

In a context suggestive of Jacques Lacan, Unamuno describes the Other as a kind of mirror in which consciousness discovers its reflection. It is when consciousness internalizes its reflection that it achieves the *serse*. According to Carlos Blanco Aguinaga, the source of this theory of being-for-others (as well as Sartre's theory) is to be found in the words of Hegel: "Self-consciousness is real only in so far as it recognizes its echo (and its reflection) in another."[36] Despite their indebtedness to Hegel, however, the two thinkers give being-for-others different ontological foundations. In Sartre consciousness arises as an internal negation of being and founds the psyche; through the Other this subjective psyche is objectified. In Unamuno consciousness arises in the presence of the Other and through him discovers both the subjective and objective dimensions of the *serse.*

Because the *serse* depends on the Other, man is fundamentally alienated. He experiences alienation both in the private and social spheres. In certain respects, therefore, the *serse* can be compared to the "practico-inert" being defined by Sartre in the *Critique.* Unamuno states: "Only in society will you find yourself; if you isolate yourself from it, you will find but a phantom of your own true self. Only in society do you acquire your total meaning, but *separate* from it" (Emphasis added).[37] It is through society that man discovers the *serse.* The *serse* is thus a kind of serialized being *(en serie).*

In a sense man in society is "other than who he is." For this reason he does not confront the Other directly in a relationship of positive reciprocity but indirectly *(de soslayo).* Man as other knows the Other as other. As in Sartre, the result of this ontological situation is not the *Mitsein* but conflict.

While critics have traced Unamuno's theory of human relations to Hegel's master/slave dichotomy,[38] his discussion of being-for-others tends to be literary rather than philosophical. "Human society," he states, "is no more than a theater troop . . . [and] the roles are distributed to us by others."[39] Unlike an actor on the stage, however, man reacts against this role, and though only a *serse,* strives to achieve what Unamuno calls the *"serlo todo."*[40] This total being would represent the fulfillment of man's ontological hunger. It is precisely because man sees the Other as an obstacle in the attainment of the *serlo todo* that human relations are negative.[41]

For Unamuno there is a contradiction at the heart of human relations that might be stated in the following terms: In the presence of the Other I am an alienated being; alone I am nothing. The Other is both my damnation and my only hope. This is because there is only the Other.

29

Knowledge

While Sartre defines knowledge as the internal negation of the In-itself which is the For-itself, Unamuno defines it as a relationship between two consciousnesses. In the act of knowing, he argues, each consciousness simultaneously names the Other and internalizes its own name as articulated by the Other. The name, which is an "object" of knowledge, is the first instance of the *serse*. The *serse*, therefore, is self-knowledge.

Though Unamuno and Sartre give knowledge different ontological foundations, they both define knowledge of the Other in terms of language. For both, moreover, the naming of the Other possesses sexual overtones, and in Unamuno in particular, the "knowing" consciousness attempts to penetrate the Other and fuse with him. "All vital knowledge presupposes a penetration, a fusion in the depths of the spirit, a fusion of the knowing spirit with the thing known; all the more so if the thing known is another spirit."[42] The ideal object of knowledge, therefore, is the *serlo todo*, in which all would be one. The real object, however, remains the *serse*. It is in terms of the *serse* as social-being that we will discover Unamuno's theory of ideas.

In the essay "Ideocracy," Unamuno defines an idea as a form and contrasts it to the being which it represents. "*Idea* is form, semblance, *species.* . . . But the form of what? Here is the mystery: the reality of which it is a form, the material of which it is a figure, its living content."[43] In Sartrean terms this living content would be the *praxis* that formulates the idea. In Unamuno, however, the idea exists as a social object and through it, man achieves a kind of serial identity. It is the source of his reification. "We tend to make with ideas a conjunctive social cement in which, like mollusks in a cluster, we are imprisoned."[44]

In "Intellectuality and Spirituality" Unamuno grounds this discussion of ideas in language. He maintains that language, insofar as it is common to everyone in general and no one in particular, is the essence of alienation.

One does not communicate what one wants to communicate. . . .

Hardly is a thought embodied in a word [*palabra*] . . . [than] it belongs to another, or rather it belongs to no one since it belongs to everyone. The flesh with which speech [*lenguaje*] is endowed is communal and external; it warps thought, imprisoning it and even overturning it and falsifying it.[45]

All man's action in the world, according to Unamuno, is verbal and all is subject to the same alienation described specifically in terms of language. "However free man may be within, insofar as he must exteriorize himself, manifest himself, speak or work, communicate with his neighbors, insofar as he must make use of his body or of other bodies, he becomes tied to their rigid laws, he is a slave."[46] In a word, then, man is free, but he lives in a world in which freedom constantly loses itself without ever achieving its ends. This, it might be said, is Unamuno's closest intuition of the practico-inert of Sartre.

Unamuno speaks of man's relation to the world as a "tragic struggle." In order to achieve the *serlo todo*, man humanizes the world. In so doing, however, he is simultaneously and proportionately dehumanized by the world.

Our life is a continual struggle between our spirit, which wants to take possession of the world, make it its own, make it itself, and the world, which wants to take possession of our spirit and make it in turn its own. . . . In this tragic struggle . . . I must avail myself of my enemy in order to subdue him and my enemy must avail himself of me in order to subdue me. . . . In the end he depersonalizes [what I do] and makes it his, and I appear other than I am.[47]

In its attempt to humanize the world and achieve the *serlo todo*, consciousness is alienated by the world and made other.

In the essay "What Is Truth?" Unamuno discusses the ramifications of the struggle between a humanized nature and a dehumanized man. In humanizing nature, he argues, man endows it with human qualities and relates to it as if it possessed human intentions. "He humanizes nature, attributing to it human qualities and purposes. . . . And hence our errors, errors which come from endowing nature and reality with a hidden intention, altogether lacking in them."[48] Though Unamuno

31

has elsewhere referred to a nothingness of things, his comment here suggests that only man is intentional. If man fails to know the real as it is, this is because he sees in it only a projection of himself. As in human relations, then, man as Other knows the real as Other.

Since the real is in fact non-intentional, the action of this "other" real (like the practico-inert of Sartre) is a pseudo action which derives from man. What Unamuno calls a "subtle magic" refers to the attempt of men of bad faith *(mentirosos)* to conceal freedom and to submit it to a determinism for which only they are responsible. "But the fact is that by some subtle magic, in some mysterious way, nature lies to liars."[49]

Truth in the final analysis is not to be found in things (since man never knows the thing in-itself) but in man. Truth is the very hunger for being revealed through the tragic sense. Unlike reason, which is social, truth is strictly individual and in a sense incommunicable. "Reason is what all of us, or at least a majority of us, agree on. Truth is something else again. Reason is social; truth, ordinarily, is completely individual, personal, and incommunicable."[50]

If truth is man as a hunger for being, reason can be compared to language. Reason in fact is the logic of social being. It arises through the Other and imprisons consciousness. Unamuno despairs of reason and through literature attempts to release from it the truth which makes it possible. Truth, however, remains inexpressible.

Dialectics

By unraveling certain "mysteries" of truth, Unamuno was able to envision a dialectic of history surpassing that of traditional philosophy. The key to the dialectic in Unamuno is to be found in his reading of Marx.

While Sartre did not undertake a serious study of Marx until the time of the *Critique*, Unamuno began his career as a Marxian Socialist. After joining the Party in the 1890s, he explained that he had been attracted to socialism because it derived from science. He had studied "scientific" socialism during his youth and eventually felt the need to commit himself to direct action: "It is not enough to remain in a region cold and isolated from the burning struggles; it is necessary to descend into the arena."[51]

In a letter to *La Lucha de Clases* Unamuno summarizes his views on Marx during the early 1890s. ". . . I have at last been filled with the conviction that socialism, clean and pure, without disguise or alteration, the socialism which Karl Marx initiated with the glorious International Workingmen's Association and to which flow currents from other places, is the only truly living ideal today."[52]

Unamuno, however, eventually abandoned Marxism. In the essay "The Idealist Conception of History" he criticizes historical materialism and argues in favor of a "historical idealism." "According to this doctrine [the doctrine of historical materialism], at the foundation of social phenomena there lies . . . the economic phenomenon. . . . This entirely deterministic and even fatalistic doctrine, culminates in that statement of Marx that it is things and not men that rule history."[53]

What Unamuno criticizes in Marx is a materialist conception of history which takes man as the object of history rather than the subject. Such a materialism, he argues, submits man to a formula and in so doing loses sight of its end. "The genuine materialist understands only what is commensurable and ponderable, what can be measured, counted, and weighed. He has an arithmetic rather than geometric conception of the world."[54]

It is Unamuno's contention that the driving force of history is not matter but man's insatiable hunger for being. In the pursuit of the *serlo todo*, however, man never knows matter as such but rather an idea of matter, or what Sartre calls "immaterial matter." "Since we have no immediate experience of matter, since what we call matter as well as what we call spirit is for us a sensation, matter is an idea. And hence materialism can in a certain sense be called idealism."[55]

Unamuno thus attempts to transcend a materialism which he considers "idealistic," envisioning what Sartre would call a realist materialism. Sartre, nevertheless, does not attribute idealism to Marx but rather to certain latter-day Marxists who, like Unamuno himself, ignore Marx's fundamental statement that it is man who makes history on the basis of existing material conditions. For Sartre this emphasis on the human moment of history not only integrates man into the dialectical process but makes a dialectic of history possible. Unamuno does not derive this consequence from his original intuition. Nevertheless, he possesses an understanding of dialectics surprisingly similar to Sartre's.

Not only does Unamuno place man at the heart of history, but he clearly establishes the interaction between man and the world. In the essay "Civilization and Culture" he states significantly: "I and the world—we make each other mutually."[56] Moreover, he argues that there is no veritable division between man and the world.

> There is an exterior environment, the world of sensible phenomena, which envelops us and sustains us, and there is an interior world, our own consciousness, the world of our ideas, fantasies, desires, and feelings. No one can say where the one ends and the other begins; no one can trace a dividing line, no one can say up to what point we belong to the external world or the external world belongs to us.[57]

According to Unamuno the interior and exterior are two moments of a dialectical process. The link between the two is the tool. As a material object with a human designation, the tool possesses both an interior and exterior dimension. He states that man uses tools (and himself as a tool) to alter his environment and that when he re-internalizes his altered environment, his level of consciousness changes.

> It can be said that the environment works on man and man on the environment, the environment on itself by means of man and man on himself by means of the environment. Nature made us make our hands; with these we created in our exterior world tools and in our interior world the use and understanding of them; the tools and their use enriched our mind and our mind thus enriched, enriched the world from which we had taken them. Tools are at once my two worlds: the one within and the one without. . . . It is important to feel with deep and living understanding this communion between our consciousness and the world and how the world is our product and how we are the product of the world.[58]

Both man and the world constantly change as the result of a dialectical process in which man is the driving force. Unamuno argues, however, that this process is not a linear progression but rather a series of contractions and expansions which consciousness effects as it internalizes and re-externalizes the world. "The linear conception . . . makes us schematize progress in a series of ascending waves. No, it is not that, it is a series of qualitative expansions and contractions. . . . By expanding and contracting, by differentiating and integrating, Nature penetrates the Spirit and the Spirit penetrates Nature."[59]

The goal of history, therefore, is the realization of man. Man is at once history itself and the product of history. "The cultivation of man is the goal of civilization; man is the supreme product of Humanity, the eternal deed of History."[60] In ontological terms, historical man unceasingly attempts to found himself as the *serlo todo*. His goal, however, cannot be achieved in the world, where he suffers the alienation of the *serse*, but only in the imaginary. In the imaginary he seeks an ideal which is impossible in the real.

Imagination

Unamuno describes imagination both as knowledge and as creation. In the first instance, imagination is the knowledge which founds the *serse*. The *serse* is specifically the image of itself which consciousness discovers in the Other and internalizes. It is also a name. On the level of knowledge, imagination and language are thus the same. They are social structures, and through them man experiences a kind of serialization.

It is in contrast to "serial" imagination that Unamuno discusses "creative" imagination.

One of the greatest misfortunes that weighs on poor, common mortals is their lack of imagination, and they lack it most who most presume to possess it, confusing it pitifully with a certain memory which brings to mind the images which are in use today and which belong to the common culture. . . .[61] Imagination in them does not go beyond imagination in the etymological sense, *mimaginatio*, that is, the faculty of *mimar* or imitating—*mi-*

35

mitare—without ever arriving at fantasy. This remains for the madmen, who are the poets, or rather the creators.[62]

Imagination is thus not only an act of knowledge but an act of creation. Creative imagination opposes the structures of the *serse* and attempts to found the *serlo todo* in which all would be one. In the essay "Plenitude of Plenitudes" Unamuno states that imagination is "the most substantial faculty, the one which brings the substance of our spirit into the substance of the spirit of things and of others."[63] Since, as Unamuno has demonstrated, the only substance behind phenomenal reality is nothingness itself, what creative imagination in fact makes possible is a "knowledge" of the nothingness of others. This knowledge, of course, is not the foundation of the *serlo todo* but merely the recognition of mutual anguish. It is a knowledge that Unamuno would call love.

Since consciousness is a nothingness that hungers for a total-being beyond its reach, it might best be described as a "dream of being." In this context fantasy and consciousness would be synonymous, and according to Unamuno we are, in the words of Shakespeare, "such stuff as dreams are made on."

The *serlo todo* for which consciousness hungers is, in the final analysis, God. Consciousness is specifically a hunger for God *(apetito de divinidad)*. Unamuno defines God as a kind of projection of the *serse* to the infinite. All human action, therefore, can be seen as a "project of becoming God."

The God envisioned by Unamuno in certain respects resembles the God described by Sartre in *Being and Nothingness*. For both, God would be an impossible synthesis of two beings: *serse/serlo-todo*, For-itself/In-itself. Meyer notes this parallel between Unamuno and Sartre. "One could compare this ontological situation of the impossibility in Sartre of a being which would be at once in-itself and for-itself, that is God. In Unamuno there is equally an 'impossibility' of equivalence of the *serse* and of the *serlo todo*."[64]

For Unamuno, God does not exist as Supreme Being but as the desire for being. Certain critics have taken this desire as proof of Unamuno's belief in the existence of God and Meyer even states: "It must be said paradoxically that *God wants to be God. . . .* God wants the impossible."[65] This desire for God, however, never succeeds in founding itself and becoming God, and the only reality remains man himself.

Critics are in fact divided over the question of Unamuno's faith. According to Antonio Sánchez Barbudo, Unamuno attempted to use religion to overcome the tragic sense, but he was never able to regain the faith of his childhood: "The truth is, and he himself stated it often, that he was not able to believe in God."[66] Antonio Regalado goes so far as to suggest that Unamuno was in bad faith and that he imagined "the existence of God, even though he was an atheist . . . and was convinced that he was passing through the dream of life from nothingness to nothingness."[67]

Though not a believer in the traditional sense, Unamuno never accepted atheism and, compared to Sartre, was a religious man. What he needed in God, however, was not a justification for being but an assurance of his own immortality. Unamuno despaired over the fact that he must die, and his desire to be God was ultimately a desire to be immortal. It might be said, therefore, that even if God existed in the here and now, Unamuno would see Him as no more than a means to his own end.

Unamuno's faith was based not on a conventional belief in God but on the hope that man might somehow transform himself into God. This in fact is how he defined faith: an act of creating *(crear)*, not an act of believing *(creer)*. Faith is the same as creative imagination, and according to Unamuno, the greatest saint is the poet: "The poet is he who gives us a personalized world, an entire world made man, the word made world."[68] Through the imaginary, the poet would thus realize the impossible dream of being: the *serlo todo,* or what Sartre calls a "maximum of being."

3. Literary Theory

The Literary Theory of Sartre

The philosophy of Sartre provides the key not only to the philosophical intuitions of Unamuno but to his literary works. Literature is Unamuno's fundamental means of expression and in a sense the confirmation of the philosophy we have heretofore attempted to articulate. In order to understand fully the meaning of this literature, however, it will first be necessary to outline Sartre's theory of literature contained in *What Is Literature?* and *The Family Idiot* and to relate it to Unamuno's. Only then will we be prepared to examine the literature that established Unamuno's reputation as Spain's foremost writer of the modern period.

What Is Literature?

Published five years after *Being and Nothingness, What Is Literature?* marked a turning point in the history of literary theory. It was in *The Psychology of Imagination* that Sartre laid the groundwork for this study. There he stated that an aesthetic object was an unreal object posited by an imagining consciousness. In *What Is Literature?* he applied this concept specifically to literature. What resulted was his now famous distinction between poetry and prose. Though less black and white than he originally suggested, this distinction made possible an understanding and discussion of what came to be known as the "commitment" of the existentialist writer.

Sartre begins *What Is Literature?* with an analysis of painting. In painting, he argues, the real object that the artist per-

38

ceives in the world undergoes a fundamental change when transferred to a canvas: it becomes imaginary. The artist grounds the imaginary object in the In-itself of an *analagon* (paints, canvas, ink, sound waves, and the like). In the aesthetic experience, the spectator-consciousness perceives the *analagon* but, through an act of "irrealization," transforms it into an aesthetic object. Once constituted, he takes this aesthetic object not as a sign of the real but as a thing-in-itself.

It is Sartre's contention that the word in poetry, like the color in painting, possesses the opacity of a thing. It is not a sign of the real but rather an essence. "The empire of signs is prose; poetry is on the side of painting, sculpture, and music. . . . In fact, the poet has withdrawn from language-instrument in a single movement. Once and for all he has chosen the poetic attitude which considers words as things and not as signs."[1]

The prose writer treats the word not as an object but as a sign. Unlike the poet, he "uses" language to reveal some aspect of the real. For him language neither precedes things nor produces them; rather, it is consciousness itself as a revelation of being. In prose "we are within language as within our body. We *feel* it spontaneously while going beyond it toward other ends."[2] Prose is utilitarian since it uses words as designations of objects. It represents a certain moment of action and always effects some change in the world.

In prose, as in all action, the writer reveals a particular situation through an attempt to change it in the light of future ends. The prose writer has chosen what Sartre calls a method of secondary action, which is "action by disclosure." Such a writer is "committed" because his words act indirectly upon reality and thrust both himself and the reader into the world. He is in good faith, and through the act of writing he accepts responsibility for the world in which he lives. "The writer has chosen to reveal the world and particularly to reveal man to other men so that the latter may assume full responsibility before the object which has been thus laid bare."[3]

Sartre maintains in *What Is Literature?* that poetry is not committed. Unlike prose, where the word is a free transcendence of being toward a future end, the word in poetry represents freedom in the form of an essence. The poet takes language not as the lived relation between consciousness and the world but as something outside of man: "There is the word which is lived and the word which is met."[4] For him the word is a substance rather than a sign, and to understand it man would have to place himself beyond the human condition, on what Sartre calls the side of God.

As Sartre explains in *The Words*, the poet lives under the same illusion as the believer. For him language possesses the infinite density of being but is at the same time self-conscious. It represents the ideal unity of the In-itself and the For-itself, the "word" made flesh, or man become God.

As in *Being and Nothingness*, Sartre explains in *What Is Literature?* that consciousness is a revealer of being but not a producer of being. It is through consciousness that being comes to be differentiated and that things have meaning but, *qua* being, consciousness remains unessential to the being of which it is conscious. Even when confronted with a "beautiful" landscape, the spectator knows that its being precedes him and that the relations which he establishes could very well be otherwise.

In art, consciousness is both a perceiver and producer of being, and through the imaginary object, it comes to see itself as essential: "One of the chief motives of artistic creation is certainly the need of feeling that we are essential in relationship to the world."[5] In fact, because of the spectator's dual nature as perceiver and producer, it may be said with regard to the aesthetic object that *esse est percipi*.[6]

Sartre holds that literature is an aesthetic object which is realized through the joint efforts of both the writer and the reader. The writer himself is unable to perceive his creation since he remains the subjectivity by which it is produced. The reader, on the other hand, both perceives the work as an object in the world and re-creates it in the imaginary. The act of reading is thus the synthesis of perception and creation.

It is Sartre's view that the author writes not for himself but for the reader. He appeals to the freedom of the reader to objectify the subjective experience of writing. The freedom of both is the *sine qua non* of the work, but it is through the reader that the aesthetic object is actually produced. Sartre calls generous any feeling which has its origin and end in freedom, and since both reader and writer demand each other's freedom, both are in a spirit of generosity.

What Sartre defines as aesthetic joy is the experience of the reader and not the writer. Its essential structures correspond to the dual nature of reading as both perception and creation. In aesthetic joy there is a positional consciousness of the object as given by the writer and a non-positional consciousness of being essential to the re-creation of the object in the imaginary. This object, Sartre explains, is the world as intended through the imaginary, but it is also a value since it is an appeal to human freedom. The transformation of the world into a value is described by Sartre as "the aesthetic modification of the human project."[7]

The commitment of literature is thus one of freedom. Sartre states. "Writing is a certain way of wanting freedom."[8] In theory, literature cannot deny freedom, for if it did so, it would deny the possibility of its own existence. It both demands and affirms freedom. For this reason it possesses an ethical dimension. It is both an aesthetic imperative and a moral imperative.

> Although literature is one thing and morality a quite different one, at the heart of the aesthetic imperative we discern the moral imperative. For, since the one who writes recognizes, by the very fact that he takes the trouble to write, the freedom of his readers, and since the one who reads, by the mere fact of his opening the book, recognizes the freedom of the writer, the work of art, from whichever side you approach it, is an act of confidence in the freedom of men.[9]

The fundamental commitment of literature is characteristic of both prose and poetry to the extent that both demand and affirm freedom. Nevertheless, the two differ in their treatment of freedom. In prose the imaginary object is the world as given, but as if it had its source in human freedom. In poetry the imaginary object is human freedom become the world. Poetry requires the freedom of the reader, but it presents freedom as if it were a thing. Poetry, therefore, simply carries

41

prose a step farther, for if in prose, as Sartre has said, man recovers the world and encloses it within himself, in poetry man and the world become one. This, of course, is an impossibility, for if a freedom became a thing, it would no longer be a freedom. Nevertheless, it is the ideal of consciousness insofar as consciousness posits the synthesis of the In-itself and the For-itself as its ultimate goal.

Although prose recognizes the freedom of the reader and in fact requires it, it does not provide for the realization of a *Mitsein* between reader and writer or between readers. Two different readers may posit the same end through their reading of a work, but this end is fundamentally imaginary and thus there exists no real reciprocity between them. "Lacking the wherewithal, the city of ends lasts for each of us only while we are reading; on passing from the imaginary life to real life we forget this abstract, implicit community which rests on nothing."[10] Reading, therefore, is not communion but rather companionship with the Other.

According to Sartre, a veritable communion with the Other is not possible at this time in history. As clarified in the *Critique,* this is because man lives in a world of scarcity where he must treat the Other as a thing if he is to survive. Sartre states: "The city of ends which, with one stroke, he has set up in the aesthetic intuition is only an ideal which we shall approach only at the end of a long historical evolution."[11] Literature, then, can neither bring down the existing structures of society nor usher in the reign of freedom. But, it can enhance man's awareness of his project of freedom.

The Family Idiot

While the philosophical foundation of *Being and Nothingness* enabled Sartre to develop his theory of literature in *What Is Literature?*, it was the *Critique* that made possible the culmination of this theory in *The Family Idiot.* So, as we have seen, the great contribution of the *Critique* is to be found in the elucidation of the structures of the "immaterial matter" of the practico-inert. It is through worked matter that man is objectified in a social environment and reduced to the status of a thing. The practico-inert, however, not only accounts for the determinism of human history but reaffirms the theory of freedom which Sartre established as the cornerstone of his entire philosophical enterprise in *Being and Nothingness*. Man can be enchained only to the extent that he is intrinsically free. The freedom of the slave is the counterpart of an ontological truth that common sense has always told us: it is impossible to enslave a stone.

Sartre's own theory of the aesthetic object in *The Family Idiot* derives from his theory of the practico-inert. As a kind of practico-inert object, the work of art is primarily worked matter. It is a thing inscribed with a human meaning. We have learned from *What Is Literature?* that the work of art is also an appeal to the freedom of the spectator-consciousness. It is in this appeal to freedom that the work of art differs from the practico-inert objects described in the *Critique*.

The work of art that Sartre discusses in *What Is Literature?* arises through the relationship between creator and spectator, but in *The Family Idiot* it is to be found explicitly in the social sphere, on the level of "objective culture." While the social constitution of the aesthetic object does not alter its fundamental ontological structure, it places it within a different context. The poetry of Baudelaire, for example, differs from the poems exchanged by two lovers in private. It comes to the spectator with meanings that are not only those of the creator but of a particular social and historical milieu. The work of art thus contains a socially instituted praxis which presents itself as such to the freedom of the spectator.

As a practico-inert object, however, the work of art differs radically from a tool. It is not an instrument used to reorganize a practical field but strictly an appeal to freedom. This difference is clarified by Sartre in his distinction between a "totality" and a "practical totality." A door, for example, on which is painted a work of a famous artist, is a practico-inert object. However, while the door and the painting are both totalities, only the door itself can be called a practical totality. The door is a socially constituted object meant to provide or prohibit access to whatever lies beyond. Though the painting is socially

43

constituted in the world of objective culture, it possesses no practical use. Works of art thus differ from other practico-inert objects in regard to their instrumentality.

Clearly, the distinction between totality and practical totality does not ignore the question of commitment raised by Sartre in *What Is Literature?* Rather, it bridges the somewhat overly rigorous division between poetry and prose that he made in that work. A musical composition, a painting, or a poem, regardless of whether or not freedom is its explicit theme, is founded on an appeal to freedom. It thus possesses what Sartre calls, in the case of Flaubert, a "mini-praxis."

Sartre crystallizes his theory of the aesthetic object in what has come to be regarded as one of the most significant statements on aesthetics in modern times. He speaks of a statue of Venus.

> I call this strange object for the first time by a name which we shall often meet subsequently: a *real, permanent center of irrealization*. . . . The being of this object is considered a permanent incitement to de-realize oneself by irrealizing this piece of marble as a Venus. The object acts as support to the irrealization, but the irrealization gives it its necessity because it is necessary that it should be if the irrealization is to take place. . . . The compact, inert being of the stone is there to be de-realized publicly while it de-realizes those who contemplate it. But forthwith something of its immutable consistency, of its radiant inertia passes into the Venus or the Pieta. This stone woman is an ideal of being, the representation of a *pour-soi* (For-itself) which could be taken for a dream of an *en-soi* (In-itself). Thus the sculptured stone, a mineral indispensable to a social irrealization, possesses certainly the *maximum of being* if we reflect that in social intersubjectivity *being* is the *être-pour-autrui* (For-others) when it is instituted.[12]

The work of art is thus a special kind of practico-inert object. It is neither the means by which man realizes himself in a practical field nor the means by which a constituted praxis realizes itself through man. Rather, it is what Sartre calls a real and permanent center of irrealization. By "derealizing" itself, consciousness "irrealizes" the aesthetic object. In the process it symbolically "realizes" the impossible In-itself-For-itself. In the aesthetic experience consciousness thus discovers what it had hoped to find in religion—the totality of being. Here, then, is the missing God of whom Sartre spoke at the end of *Being and Nothingness* and the imaginary fulfillment of man's passion as a useless being.

Sartre and Flaubert

While *The Family Idiot* provides the key to Sartre's understanding of aesthetics, it also completes his philosophical enterprise and clarifies his position as a writer. In a certain sense *The Family Idiot* was written in response to the charge of Merleau-Ponty in 1945 that *Being and Nothingness* had failed to account for the problem of passivity. In order to fill this *lacuna* in his philosophical system, however, it was first necessary to clarify the ontological structure of the practico-inert. With the philosophical instruments of the *Critique,* in addition to those of his earlier works, Sartre was then able to undertake the study of a historical figure and arrive at an understanding of passivity in a concrete human case: Flaubert.

In the preface to *The Family Idiot* Sartre reflects on his reasons for choosing to dedicate over three thousand pages to a study of Flaubert. He asks the question, "Why Flaubert?" and answers that as creator of the modern novel, Flaubert's work contains the key to all contemporary literature. In a sense Flaubert is the complete opposite of Sartre. While Sartre attempted to create the literature of commitment outlined in *What Is Literature?*, Flaubert chose to write from the perspective of poetry.[13] Yet the differences separating Sartre from Flaubert are the result of the same belief in literature and, as Sartre has revealed in *The Words,* a certain choice of the unreal over the real. It is in *The Family Idiot* that Sartre completely exposes this belief which, in the final analysis, is no more than a disguised belief in God. This final demystification of literature might be seen as the culmination of Sartre's fundamental project of atheism.

The title of Sartre's study derives in part from the young Flaubert's great difficulty in learning to read and write. Sartre finds extraordinary this state of affairs in a child who would become one of the world's greatest writers. He argues, however, that what appears to be a problem of language is the result of a more fundamental problem of being-for-others. Flaubert as a child was unloved. The product of a bourgeois family, he was taken not as an end in himself but as a duty. He was a thing to be fed and kept clean. One day he would be educated and would exercise a bourgeois profession as did his father and brother. The hands of the mother, Sartre speculates, must have held him with a kind of indifference, and because of her he would come to take himself as an object rather than a value. This would be the source of his alienation and the reason for his eventual choice of the imaginary over the real.

The alienation of the child, Sartre argues, was the cause of his extreme credulity. He was the object of the words and intentions of others but was himself never a subject. Sartre cites the amusing but peculiar anecdote of how Flaubert was once asked to go into the next room and see if he (Flaubert) was there. The child dutifully obeyed. For Sartre this reveals the extent to which the external point of view of the Other had been internalized.

If the child could take himself as a thing, it is no wonder that he would take language, the fundamental relationship between consciousness and the Other, in the same way. Sartre explains that for Flaubert words were not signs of the real but objects in themselves which he received from the Other but never made his own. Language, it might be said, "short-circuited." The result was the attitude of the poet discussed by Sartre in *What Is Literature?* It was also the attitude of the believer. Flaubert's knowledge of the world came from the Other, not from the direct relationship between consciousness and things. His world was thus an object of faith, not an object of truth.

Though Flaubert had been condemned as a child to the status of a thing, there was still, as in the case of all human beings, an ontological choice without which the power of the Other would lose its meaning. Flaubert chose passivity because the Other left him no other option. The manifestation of this choice of passivity and the key to Flaubert's entire career as a writer is to be found in the famous crisis of Pont l'Evêque.

46

It happened that Flaubert was traveling with his brother to Pont l'Evêque when he suddenly fell from his seat and collapsed at his brother's feet. According to Sartre, this incident is incomprehensible in strictly physical or psychological terms. It is in fact the result of an ontological choice—a fundamental denial of the real. In this moment Flaubert symbolically destroyed both the self and the Other. Suicide and murder. On the ruins of this world he would attempt to construct an ideal which was no more than pure illusion. We are reminded of Sartre's statement in *The Words:* "There was only one way of salvation: to die to one's self and to the World, to contemplate the impossible Ideas from the vantage point of a wreckage."[14]

Though Flaubert would symbolically murder the bourgeois family which produced and ultimately condemned him, he would remain in essence bourgeois. His rejection was in no way an attack on his class of origin but simply a moment of bourgeois negativity. What Sartre would call "neurosis art" in a sense provided a safety valve for the bourgeois class. Rather than attack the system of class exploitation, the bourgeois artist of the nineteenth century turned inward in an empty and vain search for a fulfillment that could come, as Sartre stated in *What Is Literature?*, only at the end of a long and arduous historical process.

Toward a Literary Theory of Unamuno

The Family Idiot is of particular relevance to the study of Unamuno's project as a writer. Sartre ultimately condemns the work of Flaubert insofar as it involves a choice of the unreal over the real and implicitly a belief in God. While Sartre set before himself the project of "commitment," Flaubert chose the poetic attitude. Unamuno, as we have seen, also chose to identify himself as a poet. Does this mean that Unamuno was closer to Flaubert than to Sartre in his project as a writer and in his understanding of the human condition?

In *How to Make a Novel*, Unamuno states that the work of the political activist is the same as that of the poet. Such a statement could be interpreted as a contradiction by a strict Sartrean. It is not, however, intended to suggest that politics is somehow imaginary but that poetry can in fact be committed to the struggle of freedom in the world and to the hope that man might one day achieve the fulfillment he desires. As Unamuno's philosophical writings have revealed, however, this fulfillment is not material but spiritual, and the means of achieving it are not political but in a sense religious.

It is true that Unamuno would speak out on political issues throughout his lifetime, and in *How to Make a Novel*, his philosophical comments are punctuated by criticisms of the dictatorship of Primo de Rivera, who was responsible for his exile in France. Yet, his political concerns were secondary. This does not mean, however, that his view of the world was the same as Flaubert's.

The problem of literature and the relationship between reading and writing theorized by Sartre in *What Is Literature?* is treated in literary terms by Unamuno in *How to Make a Novel*. He describes an "autobiographical" character, U. Jugo de la Raza, who was once browsing through the bookstalls along the Seine in Paris only to discover the following prophetic words: "When the reader comes to the end of this painful story he will die with me."[15] This character, to the extent that he represents Unamuno, can be taken as both reader and writer of the narration. He is like a modern-day Nebuchadnezzar, discovering his terrible fate in the written word.

It is in the context of U. Jugo de la Raza that Unamuno calls literature a kind of death. Through the written word both reader and writer inscribe themselves in the world and achieve a certain level of being. Yet in so doing they lose themselves in their object. This is the profound meaning of the Word become Letter. The result is the *serse*.

It is only by adopting a "poetic attitude" that the reader and writer might achieve the ideal being they desire. While in Flaubert the poetic attitude reduces man to the status of a word-object, in Unamuno it represents the effort to free man from the limitations of language.[16] Unamuno defines the poet as an *agonista*,[17] a victim of the tragic sense of life. Rather than accept his ontological situation, however, the poet struggles to transcend the limitations of the *serse* and to realize the *serlo todo*. Unlike the philosopher, who explains things as they are,

48

he sees himself as a kind of *poietes*, or creator of things. His task, however, is not an easy one.

> Here I am staring at these blank pages—blank as the dark future: terrifyingly blank—striving to hold on to passing time, pin down the flighty day, in short make myself eternal or immortal, although eternity and immortality are not one and the same. Here you have me before these blank white pages—my future—endeavoring to pour out my life in the hope of continuing to live, in the hope of giving myself life and tearing myself out of the hands of death every moment of the day.[18]

The words of the poet, like those spoken by Scheherazade, are a means of holding death at bay. It is a world in which art is life and all else nothingness.

Unamuno holds that style is the key to poetry and in fact to all literature. Style is not form *per se* but the individual inso far as he attempts to realize himself through a particular medium. It is in a sense the world in its interiority. "You can give me the tone and the intensity with which the world vibrates within you, the note which resounds in your heart; but you cannot give me the stamp with which you receive them, which is your own stamp. And if you transmit it to me, it is through an aesthetic sense, it is through a work of art."[19]

Style expresses itself differently in each work and, as Unamuno states, "if the poet gives . . . twenty different poems . . . he gives . . . twenty complete men."[20] The poet, it might be said, "gives of himself" and becomes his poem. He "surrenders to his creation."[21]

While the surrender of the self to rational language results in the alienation of the *serse*, the surrender to poetic language results, in theory, in the undoing of the *serse*. In the poem the poet reveals his own nothingness. Because nothingness is the being which he shares in common with all men, his work becomes a kind of communion of the anguished. In such a communion, however, man remains no more than a hunger for being. This, then, is the "missing" *Mitsein* of which Sartre spoke at the end of *What Is Literature?*

Poetry is the one genre that Unamuno and Sartre do not

share in common. Though Sartre composed several poems during his youth in the late 1920s, Unamuno wrote thousands of poems over the course of his lifetime. Most, however, reiterate in verse the philosophical problems reflected in his theoretical works. In terms of form they reflect the structure of traditional Spanish poetry and, in contrast to his novels and plays, remain within the conventions of the genre.

It is in the novel and theater that Unamuno the "poet" will express his most profound anguish and will attempt to undo the structures that thwart man in his quest for the total-being he desires. These works will not only express the existential intuitions of Unamuno but will reveal an understanding of literature radically different from that of the past. It is through the literary tradition represented by Cervantes that this "new" literature of Unamuno finds its *raison d'être*.

Unamuno and Cervantes

Both Sartre and Unamuno take as their literary models the two greatest novelists of their respective national literatures. While Cervantes is to the novel in Spain what Flaubert is to the novel in France, Cervantes is nevertheless a landmark figure in the history of European literature. It is in *Don Quixote* that Cervantes creates the modern European novel. This work possesses the fundamental characteristics that would come to define the great realist-novel of the nineteenth century. In it there exists a dialectic between the character and the world in which he lives. This dialectic presupposes two things: first, that the character is free; and second, that the world in which he lives possesses a certain logic which he can comprehend through the use of reason and eventually dominate. These two premises lie at the heart of the nineteenth-century bourgeois ideology which is reflected in the realist novel.

Though a member of the minor aristocracy, Don Quixote reveals many of the characteristics that would come to typify the nineteenth-century bourgeoisie. As an *hidalgo*, he no longer fits into the class structure of sixteenth-century Spain. His origins are in fact uncertain, and it is not until he names himself Don Quixote and attempts to become a knight-errant that we begin to know him. When he takes the windmills for giants, he is not so much questioning the meaning of reality as doing what he thinks necessary to endow himself with the identity of knight-errant which he has made his project of being. It is in the outcome of this project that the great un-answered questions of the work are to be found.

In *The Life of Don Quixote and Sancho*, Unamuno argues that the most significant moment of Cervantes' work occurs when Don Quixote meets a group of pilgrims carrying the im-ages of certain saints. Upon seeing them, Don Quixote tells Sancho that the saints have won heaven through their holy works but that his own labors have gained him nothing. It is here he realizes that the role of knight-errant which he has created for himself is not real but imaginary. In contrast to the fullness of being achieved by the glorified saints, Don Quixote remains a kind of nothingness. His experience in this moment is one of profound anguish.

Though Don Quixote knows that his ideal is imaginary, he nevertheless chooses to live as if it were real. In this context he can be compared to the protagonist of Unamuno's *St. Manuel Bueno, Martyr*, the atheistic priest who practices religion in order to spare his parishioners the anguished knowledge of their mortality in a godless universe. It is Unamuno's conten-tion in this work that the non-believer experiences the most profound suffering and becomes, paradoxically, the best Chris-tian. Through his anguish he learns a compassion for his fellow man that is comparable to that of Christ himself. In *The Life of Don Quixote and Sancho*, Unamuno argues that the "quixo-tism" of such characters is the only possible form Christianity can take in the modern world. It represents a belief that exists despite the absurdity of life and which Unamuno was wont to describe in the words of Sénancour. "Man is perishable. It well may be. But let us perish while resisting, and if nothingness is reserved for us, let us not act as if this were justice."[22]

For Unamuno it would be precisely the ability of the character to realize himself in the world through his action that would be the hallmark of the Cervantine novel. Though Don Quixote was a knight-errant only in the imaginary, he nev-ertheless created his role and in the end destroyed it when he returned home to die as Alonso Quijano the Good. Don Quixote, to be sure, is a being for the other characters but they are also beings for him.

In the novelistic works of Unamuno, on the other hand, we will find a very different situation. Here, the character will be denied the ability to realize himself even in the imaginary and will be no more than what the other characters and ultimately the author and reader determine him to be. In keeping with the philosophy of Unamuno, he will be a *serse* striving to achieve the ever-elusive and impossible *serlo todo*. In contrast to the character of the Cervantine novel, however, he will be profoundly conscious of his ontological reality. It is in this self-consciousness that we will discover man's existential freedom.

4. Novel

The Novel of Sartre and Unamuno

According to Simone de Beauvoir, the novel is of particular importance to existentialism. In her article "Littérature et métaphysique" she explains that while philosophy objectifies human reality, the novel captures it as it is lived, in all its subjective complexity and ambiguity. Only the novel, she asserts, can evoke the original upsurge of existence. This is because it presents existence not as an object of thought but as action, feeling, and experience. It is thus a unique revelation of being, irreducible to a formula or to a system of philosophy.[1]

Though her definition was meant in large measure to apply to Sartre, it is, not surprisingly, more applicable to Unamuno. In his career as an existentialist thinker, Sartre wrote only two novels, *Nausea* and *Roads to Freedom*. Unamuno, on the other hand, made the novel one of his primary means of expression. In a way similar to Simone de Beauvoir, Julián Marías argues that the novel of Unamuno provides the reader with a first intuition of human reality. It is not an abstraction of man but man himself in his lived subjectivity. It is a novel that might be taken as the point of departure in the formation of an existential ontology.[2]

Having already articulated the existential ontology of Unamuno, we are now in a position to undertake a new reading of his most significant novel and to identify in it the intuitions recognized by such critics as Marías. What we will find is not only an expression of Unamuno's philosophical concerns but

53

an understanding of the novel transcending that of the great realist novelists and indeed of Cervantes himself.

Unamuno uses the word *nivola* (as opposed to *novela*) to describe his major works of prose fiction. The *nivola* differs from the traditional novel in its understanding of human reality. The character is a *serse*. Unable to realize himself through his own actions, he is merely what the Other sees him to be. While the character of the realist novel was free to achieve his ideal and become, in the words of the bourgeoisie, a "self-made man," the character of the *nivola* is unable to fulfill his anguished desire for an ideal being which in principle is unattainable.

We have learned through Unamuno's "existential" interpretation of the work of Cervantes that Don Quixote is capable of self-realization and creates for himself, albeit in the imaginary, the identity of knight-errant. The character of the *nivola* will make no such choice regarding his being. However, he will be free to question the choices others have made for him. He will come to understand his nature as a being for the other characters and indeed for the author and the reader. It is this profound self-consciousness that will set him apart from such characters as Don Quixote and will in the end destroy the traditional structures of the novel. To the extent that the *nivola* is a novel that has become conscious of itself, we might call it an anti-novel.

In the "Prologue-Epilogue" to the second edition of *Love and Education*, Unamuno offers a definition of the *nivola* as he practiced it over many years. He explains that the theme of the *nivola* is human consciousness, which he describes as a kind of nothingness that must be endowed with being.[3] This consciousness is no more than a desire for an ideal it is not and which it will seek through the creation of personality. It is for this reason that Marías would come to speak of Unamuno's novel as a *novela personal*.[4]

We do not find in the novel of Sartre a redefinition of the genre but rather a subjective approach to the philosophical problems raised in his theoretical works. On the level of genre, Unamuno's novel is more stylistically innovative than Sartre's. Nevertheless, the philosophical system reflected in the novel of Sartre can be used to help clarify the profound meaning of the *nivola*.

Of Sartre's two novels, *Nausea* has enjoyed greater popularity and is now recognized as a classic of Western literature. While *Roads to Freedom* stands as a record of his intellectual and political concerns during the years of World War II, Sartre found himself at an impasse while writing the work and never completed it. Simone de Beauvoir would explain that because of his inability to resolve the problem of ethics undertaken after *Being and Nothingness,* he would be unable to identify the proper commitment for the freedom of the characters of *Roads to Freedom*.[5] He knew that an affirmation of freedom was an ethical act, but he did not know what form such an affirmation could or should take. It was not until the completion of the *Critique* that he found a solution to these problems.

It would be Sartre's contention that *Saint Genet* and *The Family Idiot* are in certain respects novels. Like Unamuno's *How to Make a Novel,* however, they should be defined *sui generis.* For this reason *Nausea* can rightly be taken as Sartre's most significant novel and, for our purposes, the point of departure in the study of Unamuno's *nivola*.

Nausea

The key to *Nausea* is to be found in the title of the novel. In *Being and Nothingness* Sartre defines nausea in ontological terms as the non-thetic apprehension of consciousness of its own contingency as an existent. It is through nausea that consciousness discovers its facticity: "A dull and inescapable nausea perpetually reveals my body to my consciousness."[6] While a physiological attack of nausea is experienced when the balance between the body and the environment is broken (whether through rapid movement or the ingestion of certain foods), ontological nausea is experienced when the For-itself internally negates the In-itself. The For-itself, it might be said, is a turning-over in the "belly" of being. It is in this context that the protagonist of *Nausea,* Antoine Roquentin, makes the fundamental statement: "The Nausea . . . it is I."[7]

Roquentin is a marginal figure who lives in a provincial

French city called Bouville (Mudville) and who, as the novel opens, is writing a biography on the eighteenth-century Marquis de Rollebon. He lives alone in a rented room near a train station and has no friends except for a former lover, Anny, and several acquaintances in the local cafe and library, chief of whom is the Self-Taught Man. He regards himself as an outsider, alienated from the bourgeois society around him and from his own past. His alienation is experienced in nausea, and as he gradually withdraws from his surroundings and his former self, the nausea becomes increasingly intense. Eventually, he realizes the absolute contingency of his facticity and of all existence. He discovers that while man is without justification, he is totally responsible for the meaning of his world. Aprioristic values represent no more than the vain effort of consciousness to conceal from itself the anguish of its nothingness. Roquentin learns that nausea is in fact his normal state and that recourse to the imaginary is the only possible escape from contingency. Thus, after a final understanding and acceptance of his existential condition, he decides to become a writer of literature.

It is in his reflection on the meaning of adventure that Roquentin begins to understand the fundamental difference between the real and the imaginary which will change his life forever. An adventure involves a simultaneous denial of the real and affirmation of the unreal. It is for this reason comparable to a work of art. What Roquentin had believed were adventures were in fact "aesthetic experiences."

> I have never had adventures. Things happened to me, events, incidents, anything you like. But no adventures. It isn't a question of words; I am beginning to understand. There is something to which I clung more than all the rest—without completely realizing it. It wasn't love. Heaven forbid, not glory, not money. It was . . . I had imagined that at certain times my life could take on a rare and precious quality. There was no need for extraordinary circumstances: all I asked for was a little precision. . . . And naturally, everything they tell about in books can happen in real life, but not in the same way. It was to this way of happening that I clung so tightly. (p. 37)

Like a work of art, an adventure is a totality through which the individual parts achieve meaning. According to its "internal logic," each moment is demanded by the following and in a sense the end is already present in the beginning, endowing it with a *raison d'être*. Heretofore Roquentin lived his life as if telling a story and erred to the extent that he saw events as being necessary. Now he must make a fundamental choice: "live or tell" (p. 39). It is a choice of either the real or the imaginary which, he will discover, can be made only because consciousness is free.

As Roquentin disengages himself from the imaginary, he comes to perceive the real in its fundamental nature. He awakes one morning to discover the fog. "Fog had filled the room: not the real fog, that had gone a long time ago—but the other, the one the streets were still full of, which came out of the walls and pavements. The inconsistency of inanimate objects!" (p. 76). The "inconsistency" of things of which Roquentin speaks does not represent a change in Sartre's theory of the In-itself. It is rather a metaphor for the transphenomenality of being. Though Roquentin attempts to endow being with its conventional meanings, being surpasses any meaning he might ascribe to it. The fog thus reveals the In-itself. We will see that it differs from the mist of Unamuno's *nivola*, which symbolizes the nothingness of consciousness prior to the upsurge of the *serse*.

As Roquentin lets go of the past and his conventional definition of things, he comes face to face with existence. He states: "Existence, liberated, detached, floods over me. I exist" (p. 98). Nausea, he realizes, is simply the act of "existing" his freedom. In a way similar to the protagonist of *Mist*, he struggles with Cartesian logic. He utters the words, "I think, therefore I am," in an attempt to consider himself from the standpoint of reflective consciousness. He is, however, unable to achieve a reflective scissiparity and remains the spontaneous consciousness which makes the *cogito* its object. "Existence takes my thoughts from behind" (p. 102).

Roquentin's revelation of existence reaches its climax when he enters the town's public garden. His experience there is the most profound of the entire novel, and he refers to it as an illumination. For a moment the meaning of things vanishes and he collides head on with being. "Usually existence hides itself. . . . And then all of a sudden, there it was, clear as day: existence had suddenly unveiled itself. It had lost the harmless look of an abstract category: it was the very paste of things . . ." (p. 127).

Each existent, such as the chestnut tree in the garden, exists for no reason and, although knowledge attempts to endow being with necessity, being remains absolutely contingent. Roquentin thus states: "The world of explanations and reasons is not the world of existence" (p. 129). Contingency is in fact the key to all existence. "The essential thing is contingency. I mean that one cannot define existence as necessity. To exist is simply *to be there;* those who exist let themselves be encountered, but you can never deduce anything from them" (p. 131).

Because being is fundamentally contingent, Roquentin reasons that there can be no God. The belief in God represents man's vain attempt to endow being with necessity. As he reflects on the impossibility of God, Roquentin experiences nausea—the revealing intuition of consciousness of universal contingency.

It is in this context that Roquentin's statement, "the Nausea . . . it is I," takes on its full significance. Consciousness, as existent, is no more than the revealing intuition, and as such, internal negation of being. Although it is real, it is logically subsequent to the being of which it is conscious. "This nothingness had not come *before* existence, it was an existence like any other and appeared after many others" (p. 134). For Roquentin no more can be said about existence. He leaves the garden, returns to his room, and writes down his ontological discoveries.

Although Roquentin experiences this intuition of being while alone in the garden, he is profoundly influenced by several secondary characters similar to those we will meet in *Mist*. The most important of these is Anny. Roquentin hopes to find in her a refuge from his existential unrest. Their relationship, however, is one not of harmony but conflict. Both have changed since their last separation, but Anny continues

58

to see him as the same person she formerly knew. She confides that he serves as a landmark by which she measures the changes in her own life. Based on this relationship she can be taken as the Other who attempts to reduce him to the status of a thing. Roquentin refers to her look as that of Medusa. It is the same look that the protagonist of *Mist* will experience in the presence of the woman he hopes to marry.

Another character, the Self-Taught Man, attempts to acquire universal knowledge by reading all of the books in the library in alphabetical order. He takes knowledge as an essence rather than a mode of existence, and in his private life accepts without question the definitions others have attributed to his homosexuality. In the end he allows himself to become involved in a homosexual scandal which he assumes is his inevitable destiny. It is this "essentialism" that we will find in certain of the characters of *Mist*.

While Roquentin is unable to find satisfaction with these characters, he is relieved of his sense of nausea through the act of writing. "The truth is that I can't put down my pen: I think I'm going to have the Nausea and I feel as though I'm delaying it while writing" (p. 173). Roquentin thus decides to write a novel. Unlike his work on the Marquis de Rollebon, the subject of his novel will be imaginary: "A story, for example, something that could never happen, an adventure" (p. 178). When the book is finished, he will be able to view his own past as a sort of adventure and endow it with meaning.

> But a time would come when the book would be written, when it would be behind me, and I think that a little of its clarity might fall over my past. Then, perhaps, because of it, I could remember my life without repugnance. Perhaps one day, thinking precisely of this hour, . . . I shall feel my heart beat faster and say to myself: "This was the day, that was the hour, when it all started." (p. 178)

Roquentin thus becomes a novelist. The novel which he writes is in fact the one which is now completed—*Nausea*. Its subject is no less than the adventure of consciousness in the world. By translating it into art, he has attempted to escape contingency and endow being with necessity. However, be-

59

cause his goal has only been achieved in the imaginary, he has not surpassed the "human nature" that he discovered through the ontological experience of nausea.

The character Roquentin provides further insight into Sartre's early enterprise as a writer. Sartre reveals in *The Words* that even as a child he realized heroic adventures exist only in the realm of fiction. He states: "I launched out upon a simple and mad operation that shifted the course of my life: I palmed off on the writer the sacred powers of the hero."[8] Sartre would come to see Roquentin's choice to write as proof of his own early idealism. It stands in sharp contrast to the bitter situation of Unamuno's protagonist in *Mist*, who is a hero neither in his real nor his imaginary world.

Mist

The fundamental link between *Mist* and *Nausea* is to be found in the title of Unamuno's work. It is a link, however, that both joins and separates the two thinkers in their understanding of being. While the fog in *Nausea* reveals the pure, undifferentiated being of the In-itself, the mist in Unamuno's work is indicative not of things but consciousness itself. It is Unamuno's contention that consciousness, in the absence of the Other, is a kind of nothingness. What we will discover in *Mist* is that only through contact with the Other does this nothingness take on form. We will not, however, find the profound intuition of the world of things experienced by Roquentin.

While *Nausea* and *Mist* rest on different ontological foundations, the protagonists of both works experience a crisis of being. As *Mist* opens, Augusto Pérez appears at the door of his house and, before leaving, extends his hand in order to determine whether or not it is raining. This action, though significant, is described by what it is not, as if to contrast him to the traditional hero of literature—the man of adventure envisioned by Roquentin—and show him to be ineffectual: "He was not taking possession of the external world, but merely observing whether or not it was raining."[9] When he feels rain on the back of his hand he winces, not because of the inclement weather but because he must open his umbrella. Augusto considers the closed umbrella beautiful because it is useless, and his attitude is suggestive of *fin de siècle* aestheticism. On a deeper level, however, he reveals an unfamiliarity with the meaning which things possess in a social context and which can be acquired only through others.

When Augusto leaves the house, he has no goal and tells himself that he will follow the first dog he sees. His initial encounter on the street, however, is not with a dog but a woman, Eugenia. Eugenia does not see him but her eyes attract him and awaken him from what he calls the "mist" of his existence. So it is in this moment that he is born into the world of others.

Augusto describes his existence prior to the discovery of Eugenia in terms of boredom. Although again reminiscent of the *fin de siècle* tradition, his comments regarding "vital boredom" are suggestive of Sartre. "Tedium [*el aburrimiento*] is the substratum of life, and it is from tedium that most games have been invented, games and novels—and love. Life's mist distills a bittersweet liquor which is tedium" (p. 47). According to Sartre's theoretical works boredom, along with anguish and nausea, is one of the fundamental intuitions of being. Augusto, it will be seen, experiences these fundamental intuitions: boredom before he enters into a relationship with the Other; anguish in the presence of the Other; and a kind of reverse nausea—the desire to eat—after the Other has abandoned him.

Soon after Augusto sees Eugenia on the street, the dog Orfeo appears. Orfeo is an important figure in the book and will be present during most of Augusto's soliloquies. While the dog is taken by Alexander Parker as a symbol of the childhood self from which Augusto has become separated by his awakening sexuality,[10] on a more philosophical level he can be seen to indicate the beginning of reflexivity in Augusto. Unamuno emphasizes that the dog is a non-linguistic, non-rational creature, and hence, within the context of his ontology, not a *serse*. Rather, he is the "pre-historical" Augusto, who has neither been known by the Other nor knows himself. Because of Eugenia, however, Augusto is becoming a *serse* and discovering himself as a being-for-others. Through Orfeo he experiences

being-for-itself. He is no longer himself in the form of an identity ("in-itself") but "self-conscious."

Augusto's introduction to Eugenia is preceded by an event
that foreshadows the course his relationship with her will
take. As he passes in front of her house one day a bird cage falls
from her window, hitting him on the head. In the light of Unamuno's social theory, the cage symbolizes the world of human
relationships in which the individual achieves a kind of being
at the expense of his freedom.

When Augusto enters Eugenia's house, he is first met by
her Uncle Fermín and Aunt Ermelinda. Fermín explains his
views concerning human freedom. He describes himself as a
"mystical anarchist" whose goal is the liberation of man from
all alienation and the attainment of a higher being. Ermelinda,
on the other hand, opposes freedom and defends the structures
that enchain it, although her criticism of anarchism is no more
than a tautology: "What a piece of nonsense! Imagine: no one
in command, no one giving orders. If no one gives orders, who
is going to obey?" (p. 59).

Fermín and Ermelinda later express their views on freedom in the context of love. According to Ermelinda, if a relationship between two people is to be real, it must be founded
on a knowledge that begins with the "look." While Fermín recognizes that human relations are based on knowledge, he says
that it should be a "penetrating knowledge" which would produce a kind of *Mitsein*. Fermín thus represents an individual
desire for a total-being which could be achieved only through
love. Ermelinda, on the other hand, represents the point of
view of society, where freedom is alienated and ultimately objectified in the *serse*. As might be expected, Augusto's relationship with Eugenia, and indeed with all the characters, will
develop according to Ermelinda's definition of human relations.

When Eugenia and Augusto finally meet in the house of
her aunt and uncle, it is through the "look" that their relationship is defined. Augusto's eyes are compared to those of a
hungry dog begging for food. Through love he hopes to overcome his existential nothingness and experience a fullness of
being. Her look, however, is not a "blessed rain which dissi-

pates and condenses the mist of daily existence" (p. 64) but an act of aggression. She stares into his eyes and he begins to lose consciousness and become a thing. "The poor man now really was overcome. His heartbeat quickened, his face reddened. He could scarcely make out Eugenia's eyes behind a sudden red mist. He thought he was losing consciousness" (p. 85). As in Sartre, the color red symbolizes the shame which consciousness experiences when it is seen by the Other and reduced to the status of a thing.

While Augusto discovers himself to be the object of the look of Eugenia, his initial comment to the ironing-girl, Rosario, reveals her to be the object of his look: "I've never seen you get so red of a sudden. . . . And besides, you suddenly seem a changed girl" (p. 91).[11] Augusto's relationship with Rosario possesses from the outset an erotic dimension absent from his relationship with Eugenia. This, however, is not the result of the inaccessibility of Eugenia but of the tripartite nature of his desire. Augusto will come to describe three levels of consciousness—the head, the heart, and the stomach—and will conclude that Eugenia arouses his mind's desire, Rosario his heart's, and the maid, Liduvina, his stomach's.

Augusto becomes aware of his ontological reality not only through the female characters but the conversations with his friend, Víctor. Víctor reveals that in order to forget his own personal problems, he has begun to write a novel. He explains that, like *Don Quixote*, his novel will contain interpolated tales. It will not, however, be based on a preconceived plan but will create itself as he writes. The hallmark of his novel will be dialogue rather than description and, as in the theater, his characters will reveal themselves through what they say.

When he informs Augusto that he will call his work a *nivola*, we begin to wonder if Víctor is a character in the narration or if he is to *Mist* what Cide Hamete is to *Don Quixote*. In explaining the meaning of the word "*nivola*," he tells how the poet Manuel Machado, after reading one of his sonnets to Edouard Benot, exclaimed: "It's not a sonnet, it's a *sonite*" (p. 130). He does not offer an explanation of the meaning of *sonite* but suggests that his *nivola* will somehow involve the recreation of an established literary genre. It is important to note, however, that he momentarily forgets the name he has selected: "What did I call it? A *navilo* or *nebulo* . . . no, not that, a *nivola*! That's it, a *nivola*!" (p. 130). This comment, through the juxtaposition of the words *nebulo* (cloudiness) and *nivola*, suggests that the concept of "mist" is not only the key to the particular work that bears its title but to Unamuno's entire perception of the novelistic genre.

Víctor further explains that he will make one of the characters in his *nivola* a dog, so that when the protagonist is alone, there will be another present to whom he can direct his monologues. It is then that Augusto wonders if his own world is a *nivola* and if he is anything more than the dream of some Other, whether it be God or an unseen author. As he achieves this reflexive knowledge of himself as a character of fiction, we begin to realize the significance of *Mist* in the development of the European novel. *Mist* is not a metaphor for a moment of history but a real moment in a dialectical process when literature as "*historia*" becomes self-conscious.

It is in the context of his conversations with Víctor that Augusto clarifies his ontological reality to himself. He states: "Every one of us does nothing but act out his role in life. We're all so many characters in a drama, mere masks, actors!" (pp. 135–36). He realizes that his role has been conferred upon him by Eugenia. It is a role he has internalized and that has come to identify him. "As if I were a puppet, a dupe, a Little Mr. Nobody. But I have a personality, too, yes I do, I am I, myself! Yes I am. I am I, myself! And I owe that to Eugenia. Why deny it?" (p. 142).

In solitude Augusto imagines that he controls the being with which he has been endowed. He remains, however, an object for the Other, and when he enters the social sphere, he experiences complete alienation. "Only when he was by himself was he conscious of who he was. Only then could he say, perhaps to convince himself, that 'I am I, myself!' When he was thrown among the masses, lost in the plodding, indifferent crowd of humanity, he did not have any realization of himself" (p. 143).

In an effort to control his personal relationships, Augusto turns to a certain Don Antolín Paparrigópulos, who is known for his work on feminine psychology. This ridiculous-sounding Greek name reveals a lack of respect on the part of Unamuno for classical, rational thought. Paparrigópulos is described as a seeker of rational truth, but like other such characters in Unamuno's works, and like the Self-Taught Man in Sartre's *Nausea*, he ignores the truth of man's existential reality. He contends that women either have no soul or one collective soul. He rationalizes that when Augusto fell in love with one woman, he fell in love with all women. Despite its apparent absurdity, this analysis of Paparrigópulos is correct to the extent that through love Augusto has become a *serse* and has entered the social world where all are other and hence all the same.

The interview with Paparrigópulos proves to be useless. Eugenia loves another man, Mauricio, and when Augusto learns in a letter that she intends to marry him, he experiences a mixed reaction. On the one hand he feels shame for having been deceived and ridiculed. At the same time he feels a certain indifference that causes him to question his own existence. "'If I were really like other men, if I had a heart—if I were even human, if I truly existed—how would I be able to endure this blow with the indifference I've displayed?' And unconsciously he began to touch and pinch himself to see if he felt anything" (p. 207).

With the loss of Eugenia, however, Augusto is overcome by the anguish of nothingness. He is no longer the object of her "look" and it is for this reason that he begins to experience an undoing of the *serse*. "He felt as if his soul had been shriveled up. Then he burst into tears, and he wept and wept. His thoughts finally evaporated into a fit of silent weeping" (p. 208).

The ontological problem presented in *Mist* is further developed in what would come to be one of the most famous scenes in all of Spanish literature. After Eugenia abandons him, Augusto internalizes the negative reciprocity of human relations and decides to commit suicide. He is told by Víctor, however, that he must first consult with the author of his fictional world who, it happens, is a famous "expert" on suicide. Following this reasoning, Augusto visits Unamuno, but we realize that his motives are more complicated. In his conversations with Víctor he has been informed that as a character of fiction he exists not only as a being for the other characters but as a being for the author of the work. Unamuno is thus a kind of absolute Other, and though Augusto's visit could be interpreted as an attempt to make peace with his maker before dying, it is in fact more suggestive of Jacob's struggle with the angel. What he ultimately desires is neither the permission to kill himself nor the peace of the grave, but the ideal being which he has been denied through his relations with the other characters.

It is in this context that Augusto appears in the study in Salamanca where Unamuno is composing *Mist*. In the ensuing dialogue, both the author and the character are presented as beings-for-the-other. At first Unamuno reveals a complete knowledge of Augusto's life. He alerts him to the fact that he cannot commit suicide because he is no more than a figment of an author's imagination. Despite his supposed unreality, however, Augusto is able to turn on Unamuno, his creator, and challenge his statements.

> Look here, Don Miguel . . . are you sure you're not mistaken and everything that's happening to me is the exact reverse of what you think and have told me? . . . Could it not possibly be, my dear Don Miguel, . . . that it is you and not I who are a creature out of fiction, the person who actually does not exist, who is neither living nor dead? Could it not possibly be that you are a mere pretext for bringing my story to the world. . . . (p. 219)

While Unamuno has suggested in *The Life of Don Quixote and Sancho* that the character of a novel may be more real than the author, the protagonist of *Mist* becomes aware of this possibility. Augusto confronts Unamuno with a question that Don Quixote never put to Cervantes: "What really exists, he as the consciousness that dreams or the dream itself?" (p. 220). We begin to see that this gradual *prise de conscience* in fact reveals a freedom unknown to the characters of previous works of fiction.

In keeping with Unamuno's understanding of *serse*, the relationship between Unamuno and Augusto is characterized by hostility and aggressiveness. Unamuno makes it clear that Augusto is his object and that his fate is in his hands. Augusto, however, attempts to turn the tables and make Unamuno an object for him. He looks into Unamuno's eyes and warns that the character could just as well kill the author. By the end of their conversation, however, it is apparent that Augusto is powerless to save the life he had previously intended to take. He leaves, but not without the following warning for both author and reader of the *nivola*.

> "Very well, my lord creator, Don Miguel de Unamuno, you will die too! You, too! And you'll return to the nothingness from which you came! God will cease to dream you! You will die, yes, you will die, even though you don't want to. You will die, and so will all those who read my story, every one, every single one, without a single exception! They are all fictional beings, too, creatures of fiction like myself! They will all die, each and every one! It is I, Augusto Pérez who tells you this. I Augusto Pérez, a creature of fiction like yourselves, who are as 'nivolistic' as you. Because you, my creator, my dear Don Miguel, are nothing more than just another 'nivolistic' creature, and the same holds true for your readers, just as it does for Augusto Pérez, your victim." (pp. 226–27)

When Augusto returns home, he makes a last effort to endow himself with the being he lacks. He refers to himself as a kind of nothingness—"a bottomless barrel" (p. 232)—, which through eating will be literally filled. It is in this context that he rearticulates the Cartesian maxim: *"Edo, ergo sum"* (p. 230). After consuming an excessive amount of food, however, he dies. This death is neither a suicide nor the result of overeating. Rather, at the moment when Unamuno chooses, Augusto ceases to exist. Augusto finally recognizes his dependence on Unamuno in a letter which he leaves for him: "It has all turned out as you said. You have had your way. I am dead" (p. 233).

The entire episode between author and character reconfirms Unamuno's fundamental understanding of human relations. Nevertheless, its ramifications transcend the novel itself. Not only the author is brought into the action but ultimately the reader. The reader is, as Víctor has suggested to Augusto, the unseen Other who haunts the characters' every action. Through the process of reading, the reader brings form to the "mist," giving birth to the characters (including the character Unamuno) when he imagines them alive and killing them when he imagines them dead. He then is the real assassin and in the end he will be the real victim—precisely because he alone is real.

If *Mist* is an anti-novel to the extent that it is a novel which has become conscious of itself as such, this is because its veritable subject is neither Augusto, nor Víctor, nor Unamuno, but the reader's freedom. While in the Cervantine novel the reader allowed himself to be deceived into believing in the autonomy of the characters, he becomes aware in *Mist* that they all depend on him. The *prise de conscience* that we have seen in the character, therefore, has more accurately been the reader's. It has been accompanied, however, by the tragic sense for, as Augusto has warned, the reader himself may be real only insofar as he imagines the characters and may cease to exist when God or some unseen other stops imagining him.

The *nivola* thus brings the reader to a greater understanding of his existential condition. We might ask, however, where it leaves the author. Through his transformation into a character of fiction Unamuno has attained a kind of "immortality." In the process he has become an object for his readers. He has not realized the *serlo todo* but rather reconfirmed the ontological structures of the *serse*. While in the *nivola* he becomes profoundly aware of this truth, it is in the theater that he will attempt to undo the structures of the *serse* in the hope of realizing the ideal for which he hungers.

5. *Theater*

The Theater of Sartre and Unamuno

The concept of theater is fundamental to an understanding of both Sartre and Unamuno. Founded on the spoken word, theater, rather than the novel, is the genre most suited to the expression of their respective ontologies. Action in the theater is above all language, while movements and gestures are secondary. In the ontology of Sartre language is synonymous with being-for-others. It is both original freedom and the objectification of freedom. In the ontology of Unamuno language is the constituent element of the *serse*. Because these ontological structures are the result of a negative reciprocity, we should not be surprised to find a theater of conflict in the two dramatists.

While Unamuno defines language as the essence of alienation, Sartre uses language to reveal the existence which precedes all essence. Each of his characters arises through language as a being for the other character; yet each remains fundamentally free. Sartre contends that freedom is more effectively revealed in the theater than in the novel. While the narrator of a novel gives a "second-hand" account of the characters' (or his own) action, the actor gives a "live" performance before an audience. Though his role is artificial, the portrayal seems spontaneous and natural. The spoken dialogue thus comes to represent a moment of free action in the world.

In the theater of Sartre, a well-constructed plot is less important than the performance. What matters is that the actor appear in a situation wherein he must choose a project of

69

being. Sartre refers to this as a "limit-situation." A limit-situation might be described as the facticity of the freedom that symbolically discovers itself on the stage and commits itself to a particular course of action. The first instance of a limit-situation is character. Though strictly speaking freedom and character cannot be separated, character appears to follow the freedom which makes it possible. It is in this respect that Sartre states: "The character comes later, after the curtain has fallen. It is only the hardening of choice, its arteriosclerosis, it is what Kierkegaard called *repetition.*"[1]

Because Sartre emphasizes the freedom of his characters rather than the limitations of their existence, his plays may be considered optimistic. In accordance with his philosophy, he rejects the pessimism of psychological and materialistic determinism which takes man as a thing. He does not, however, produce what would come to be known as *nouveau théâtre.* His style and technique remain conventional, and it is on the level of ideas, rather than form, that his most notable innovations are found.

While the theater of Sartre will provide us with an ontological key to the theater of Unamuno, we will find that Unamuno in fact possesses a more radical concept of the genre which in certain ways prefigures the anti-theater of the mid-twentieth century. It is in the play *Soledad* that Unamuno introduces the term *druma* to describe his particular understanding of theater. *Druma,* it will be seen, differs from drama in the same way that the *nivola* differs from the novel. In the *druma* the character achieves a profound self-consciousness. He realizes that his role is no more than a being for the other characters, the audience, and the playwright. He desires, however, a total-being which would transcend his limitations. In an effort to endow himself with this being, he attempts to destroy himself as a *serse.* In so doing he symbolically destroys the theater itself.

Through one of his characters Unamuno states: "I want something that explodes, that goes beyond the stage . . . Author, actor, and audience. . . ! Father, Son and Holy Spirit! And one true God . . . Me!"[2] While the character of the *druma* rebels against the role that has been assigned him—the sen-

70

tence that "All the world's a stage"—, he is doomed never to achieve the being he desires because of his underlying flaw— nothingness. For this reason the *druma* could be classified as a tragedy. It must be kept in mind, however, that for Unamuno the mere existence of man's quixotic desire for ideal being is a kind of victory that transcends his tragic situation.

The *druma par excellence* of Unamuno is *The Other*. As the title suggests, the play confronts the ontological problem of being-for-others. It is interesting to note that Sartre's most famous play, *No Exit*, was originally titled *The Others (Les Autres)*. The two plays are surprisingly similar, especially in regard to the use of such symbols as the mirror. A brief introduction to Sartre's play will thus help to explain the meaning of what is generally considered the most enigmatic and difficult work of Unamuno.

No Exit

No Exit is a one-act play in which the three principal characters, Garcin, Inez, and Estelle, are dead and in hell. In this hell a final and endless drama of being-for-others is enacted. The characters make a desperate attempt to gain salvation only to discover that each is the other's hell and so it must be for all eternity. Sartre's pronouncement that "hell is—other people"[3] struck its war audiences of 1944 with a ring of authentic doom and propelled him into the notoriety he was to enjoy all of his life. Viewed from the perspective of more than forty years, the play's poignancy remains unchanged.

Sartre's definition of death is essential to an understanding of the play. While Unamuno describes death in terms of individual annihilation, Sartre defines it as a facet of being-for-others. It is, he states, "the triumph of the point of view of the Other over the point of view *which I am* toward myself."[4] The dead in fact continue to change, but only as a result of the action of the living. "The dead life is . . . *all done*. . . . Nothing more can *happen* to it inwardly; it is entirely closed; nothing more can be made to enter there; but its meaning does not cease to be modified from the outside."[5]

When the characters of *No Exit* arrive in hell, they are not "absolutely" dead because they are still remembered by the living. However, though they have access to the minds of the living, they are unable to exert control over them and remain completely passive. For the time being, they are part of what Garcin calls the "public domain." Absolute death comes only when the living cease to remember them.

The first of the three characters to arrive in hell is Garcin. As the play opens, a valet leads him into a room where the distinguishing feature is a large bronze statue. Garcin asks the valet if all the rooms in hell are the same and the valet responds that they differ according to their occupants. While we know from *Being and Nothingness* that "place" for Sartre is revealed through the free choice an individual consciousness makes in the light of its future ends,[6] the characters in *No Exit* are dead and have no future since they are the In-itself being to which a living consciousness is present. Thus, they are fixed in a particular place and like the statue have become solid and inert.

When Garcin is informed by the valet that he will never again sleep, he realizes that he has entered eternity. He describes it as "life without a break" (p. 5). He learns that he will not only remain awake forever but will never again blink his eyes. He will become an empty look, and unlike the living he will be unable to reflect upon himself. It is the absence of mirrors in the room which symbolizes this impossibility of reflexivity.

While the mirror for Unamuno symbolizes the other consciousness through which consciousness discovers the *serse*, in Sartre's "realist" ontology it represents the thing which the For-itself encounters in the circuit of ipseity. The image in the mirror is the Ego and it is apprehended by consciousness as something in the world. In death, however, there can be no mirrors since the characters have become this Ego and are no longer separated from themselves by their own nothingness.

The mirror is first mentioned during the initial conversation between Inez and Garcin. Inez suggests to him that it will be easy to recognize the torturers of hell by the fear in their faces. She knows from her own experience that it is fear of the Other which motivates the sadist, and she reveals that

she has seen this fear in her own image in the mirror on count
less occasions. Garcin then informs her that anything resem-
bling a mirror has been removed from the room.

When Estelle enters the room, she immediately expresses
a desire to see herself in a mirror. Though vain about her appearance, she is assured of her existence only through a mirror:
"When I can't see myself I begin to wonder if I really and truly
exist. I pat myself just to make sure, but it doesn't help much"
(p. 19). Her behavior is reminiscent of Augusto Pérez.

To compensate for the absence of the mirror, Inez invites
Estelle to look into her eyes in order to find her reflection. But,
Estelle is unable to grasp her image there as in a mirror. This is
because Inez represents not only the In-itself of death but, as a
metaphor for the living, a human consciousness. Through her,
Estelle experiences her objectivity. As with the characters of
Unamuno, the source of this being is the Other and not herself.
Her experience is thus one of malaise and discomfort. "You
scare me rather. My reflection in the glass never did that; of
course, I knew it so well. Like something I had tamed. . . . I'm
going to smile, and my smile will sink down into your pupils,
and heaven knows what it will become" (p. 21). The absence of
a mirror distinct from the Other leads us to realize that this
Sartrean hell is much like the world of the *serse* as conceived
by Unamuno.

For the three characters of *No Exit*, as for those of Unamuno, being-for-others is inescapable. Since they are dead,
they are unable to assume control of this being by reflecting
upon themselves. Each is thus only what the other sees him or
her to be. Inez articulates the terrible reality of being-for-others
and warns Estelle that without her, she would be nothing.
"Suppose the mirror started telling lies? Or suppose I covered
my eyes—as he is doing—and refused to look at you, all that
loveliness of yours would be wasted on the desert air. No, don't
be afraid, I can't help looking at you, I shan't turn my eyes
away" (pp. 21–22).

Garcin describes Estelle's look as slimy and says to her: "I
won't let myself get bogged in your eyes. You're soft and slimy.
Ugh! . . . Like an octopus. Like a quagmire" (p. 42). His disgust
with her reminds us of the passage in *Being and Nothingness*

73

where Sartre calls slime the agony of the For-itself and the revenge of the In-itself.[7] Sartre describes slime as a sort of intermediate being which possesses neither the fluidity of consciousness nor the solidity of things. In contrast to the In-itself-For-itself, which is the ultimate value of the For-itself, slime symbolizes an attack on the For-itself by the In-itself that will eventually culminate in death. For this reason slime is an antivalue.[8] It is specifically through the Other that the characters of *No Exit* experience it.

Since each character is a trap in which the other is caught, it is in self-defense that each attempts to objectify the other in a specific role. To do this, however, they must pry into each other's lives and discover the essence each had forged in life. What they discover is that Garcin was a coward, Inez a lesbian, and Estelle an adulteress. As they learn the truths of their respective lives, however, the spectator is confronted with an ethical problem.

On the level of plot, it is not because of cowardice, lesbianism, or adultery that the three characters are now in hell but because in life they were wantonly cruel to others. It is for this reason that they could be called immoral. While Sartre's concerns in *No Exit* are ontological rather than ethical, it is difficult to separate ontology from ethics precisely because he defines being-for-others as an act of aggression against the ontological integrity of the Other. The characters in *No Exit* are doomed to live out for all eternity the negative reciprocity of being-for-others because they chose it in their relationships with others in life. This, it might be said, is their punishment. Because they could not have chosen otherwise, however, hell in a sense is inevitable. The ontological situation expressed here is thus more similar to Unamuno's than the strictly theoretical works of the two thinkers have led us to believe. In both cases, however, it leaves unresolved the ethical problem it raises.

The decisive moment of the play occurs when the characters are given the opportunity to escape from each other and perhaps even from hell. Garcin, who would rather be subjected to instruments of torture than to the look of either Estelle or Inez, cries out in a moment of desperation for release. Suddenly the door of hell swings open. This is the great *coup de théâtre*.

It is a solemn, empty moment, symbolic of consciousness it-self, a moment of freedom and choice, but frozen in the In-itself of death. In dismay the characters look beyond the gaping door towards the unknown labyrinths of hell. Then Garcin closes it, and Inez breaks into a fit of laughter. "The barrier's down, why are we waiting? . . . But what a situation! It's a scream! We're—inseparables!" (p. 43).

The fact that the door opens by itself illustrates Sartre's contention that man is not simply free but condemned to be free. It is important to note, however, that though none of the characters opens the door, it is they who close it. As dead con-sciousnesses they cannot do otherwise since they are no longer free to modify the being which they have become. As symbols of the living they are in bad faith because they choose to deny their freedom. The play's French title, *Huis-clos* (closed door), thus refers to the door of freedom, which is kept sealed by the actions of the characters.

It is in this context that Garcin expresses the theme of *No Exit* and of Sartre's understanding of human relations in gen-eral. "So this is hell. I'd never have believed it. You remember all we were told about the torture-chambers, the fire and brimstone, the 'burning marl.' Old wives' tales! There's no need for red-hot pokers. Hell is—other people!" (pp. 46–47). The Other is hell because through his look consciousness is robbed of its freedom and reduced to the status of a thing. Within the play the bronze statue symbolizes the object that the characters have thus become. Garcin states: "This bronze . . . I'm looking at this thing on the mantelpiece, and I under-stand that I'm in hell" (p. 46).

Though the characters are in hell, their world can be com-pared to that of the living since in both, the Other is forever present and inescapable. In both worlds freedom finds its limit where the freedom of the Other begins. Though Sartre would alter his theory of human relations in the *Critique*, this funda-mental tenet of his philosophy would remain unchanged.

As we have seen, the play involves a certain problem of logic. Is it possible, on the symbolic level, for the dead to speak if in death consciousness returns to the In-itself and is an abso-lute object for the Other. To raise such questions perhaps undermines the great dramatic effect of *No Exit*. It nevertheless helps us to inquire more deeply into the thought of Unamuno. If, as Unamuno holds, man is born as an object for the Other, does freedom exist? Is the *serse* possible in logical terms or is it the result of the same "error" Sartre commits when he makes the "dead" speak.

What we will discover through an analysis of *The Other* is a freedom that is unable to avoid objectification as a *serse* yet is capable of destroying it. It is a freedom even more radical than that revealed through the self-consciousness of Augusto Pérez. This freedom, which we found articulated in Sartre's theoretical works, lies at the heart of Unamuno's entire enterprise as a thinker and a writer.

The Other

When the curtain rises on the first scene of Unamuno's play *The Other*, the audience finds itself in a world markedly different from the hell of *No Exit*. It is a world where rigorous determinism and profound freedom paradoxically coexist. In *No Exit* the characters are forever fixed in their roles; in *The Other* the protagonist manages to undo his role. In the process, however, he annihilates himself. We are reminded of Sartre's introduction to Nathalie Sarraute's *Portrait of a Man Unknown*.[9] If the characters drop their masks, all that will remain is nothingness.

The Other is subtitled a "Mystery in Three Acts and an Epilogue" and is described by Unamuno as the result of his obsession with the problem of man's individual identity. Most of the significant action occurs prior to the first scene—the initial love of the identical twin brothers Cosme and Damián for Laura; the wedding of Cosme and Laura and the subsequent wedding of Damián and Damiana; and the murder of one of the brothers by the other. The play itself is a meditation on the mystery regarding the identity of the murderer and the victim.

It is essential to note that neither Cosme nor Damián appear in the cast of characters. Instead, there is only a single figure who is described as "The Other."[10] Laura, however, is identified as the wife of Cosme while Damiana is the wife of

Damián. Thus, even before the action begins, we are led to sus-
pect that there is only one male figure and that Cosme and
Damián are simply two dimensions of the same personality.

In the first act of the play, The Other describes to Laura's
brother, Ernesto, the death which has taken place. He explains
that he was sitting in his study when he suddenly saw a mirror-
reflection of himself enter the room. As he looked into the eyes
of the image before him, he began to experience a kind of
dying, or rather what he calls an "unliving" of his entire life.

> I felt myself becoming unconscious, my soul turned to water. I
> began to live—or rather to un-live—backwards, in retro-active
> time, as in a film run backwards. . . . I began to live backwards,
> toward the past, like a horse reined in and backing up. . . . And
> my whole life passed before me and once again I was twenty years
> old, and then ten, and five, and I became a child. A child! And
> then, when I could taste the milk from my mother's breast, the
> sacred milk of the breast on my innocent infant's lips . . . I was
> un-born . . . I died . . . I died when I reached the age of birth, the
> age of our birth.[11]

As in No Exit, the key to this scene and to the entire play is
to be found in the mirror. We know that in Unamuno the mirror is a symbol of the "other" consciousness through which
consciousness discovers the serse. It is Unamuno's theory that
the serse is the reflection of consciousness in the Other.
Though this reflection is the only concrete being to which consciousness can lay claim, it is an alienated being that is experienced in anguish. It is in this context that The Other states:
"Ever since we were small I've suffered at seeing myself outside myself. . . . I couldn't stand that mirror image. . . . I
couldn't stand being outside myself. . . . The way to hate
oneself is to see oneself outside oneself, to see oneself as someone else" (p. 272). Through the murder he has committed, The
Other has thus attempted to overcome the anguish of being a
serse by destroying his image in the mirror, that is, his being-
for-others. However, because Unamuno identifies being-for-
others with being-for-itself, this murder will amount to a kind
of suicide.

It is precisely through the symbol of the mirror that the

equivalence of murder and suicide is expressed in the play. In the first scene of the third act, the exact middle of the play, The Other appears and moves to the back of the stage where he uncovers a mirror. In silence he looks at his image in the mirror and menacingly extends his hands as if to attack it. However, when he sees two hands coming out of the mirror toward him, he stops and places them on his neck as if to strangle himself. Finally, he collapses at the foot of the mirror in tears. The murder/suicide symbolized here is that of the brothers Cosme and Damián. It is also that of the theater itself, which for Unamuno is by definition the *serse*.

On the level of plot it is impossible to know whether The Other is Cosme or Damián. He himself states: "I'm not Damián . . . I'm not . . . Cosme" (p. 276); and in another place: "I don't even know who I am" (p. 273). The problem of identity is never resolved and all that can be said is that The Other is, as his name implies, always and only other than who he is.

On the level of ontology the two brothers symbolize the inseparable dimensions of the *serse*: being-for-others and being-for-itself. The question arises, however, as to the identity of the "real" Other, that is, the "mirror" in whom he found himself alienated and from whom he wished to escape. This Other, as might be expected, is the female figure, and like The Other, she too reveals herself in terms of a duality.

With the two women, The Other (Cosme/Damián) appears both active and passive. In his relationship with Laura he is described as the "seducer" while in his relationship with Damiana he is described as the "seduced one." It is in this transition from the seducer to the seduced that The Other goes from objectifier to objectified. Herein, then, we find the subject/object dichotomy of human relations.

The ontological statement of Unamuno is further developed by the sexual dynamics of the different relationships. As aggressor, Damiana has "possessed" Damián and in a sense robbed him of his being. This being is symbolized by the offspring she is about to bear. The irony, of course, is that it is never really hers and will eventually escape her in its own otherness.

Throughout the play the brothers Cosme and Damián are

compared to Cain and Abel. While the Cain/Abel theme can be seen in any work which contains a fratricide, there are certain fundamental differences between *The Other* and the Genesis narration. [12] The Other is a Cain figure because of the symbolic murder he has committed. As such he wears a mark on his forehead. In contrast to the Biblical character, however, he has been marked not by God but by the human other. At first Laura pretends to have placed the mark on his forehead in order to claim him as "her" Cosme. Later, Damiana reveals that only she could have marked him since it is in her relationship with him that the woman is active and the man passive.

> DAMIANA: I can see it through your clothes . . . the mark I put on you, my own marking!
> THE OTHER: Really? What mark? What marking?
> DAMIANA: The mark of my own! (p. 280)

The mark thus symbolizes Damiana's possession of The Other. This essence, which has come to identify him through his human relationships, is not a spot on his forehead but the *serse* itself.

As the play draws to a close, Damiana claims a triumph over The Other. She insists that she possessed both Cosme and Damián as they are both dimensions of the individual she knew: "I had the two of you, I took my pleasure with both of you, you and the other one, and I deceived you both" (p. 282). According to The Other, however, she knew only the passive one, the object-self or being-for-others. "That's what you thought. But both of us agreed to deceive you even while we pretended to believe in your little game. And you had only one of us" (p. 282). It is the character's contention that being-for-others can be separated from being-for-itself. We know, however, that he is mistaken precisely because the murder of the object-self equates to the suicide of the subject-self.

Although The Other has symbolically destroyed the *serse*, Cosme and Damián remain present as long as he continues to speak. The death, in fact, has not occurred in a single blow but is rather in progress. The Other refers to the body he claims to have buried in the basement and states: "He's down there, in the dark, *dying* in the dark" (p. 259 [emphasis added]).[13] The play thus reflects the moment of death itself, and the apparent confusion is precisely the result of its temporal dissociation. It is the moment when the intimate relationship between human beings is being revealed and undone; it is what Damiana calls the "moment of total truth" (p. 282).

The actual suicide of The Other occurs offstage. This is the decisive moment prefigured in the earlier scene with the mirror. As has been seen, it is not only a suicide but the murder that The Other described to Ernesto. Before dying, The Other reveals himself to the "Other" (Laura/Damiana) in his double dimension of Cosme and Damián.

> THE OTHER: *(Within)* Laura!
> LAURA: It's *his* voice.
> THE OTHER: *(Within)* Damiana!
> DAMIANA: *That's* his voice.
> THE OTHER: *(Within)* Damiana! You can have our accursed seed, we leave it to you. More Others. . . . The furies . . . the furies! Death to Cain! Death to Abel! Die by key, die by mirror! (p. 289)

The key and the mirror mentioned in The Other's last speech can be related to the initial description of his dwelling place as a jail and a madhouse. The jail is the world of the *serse*, which arises through the "Other" (the mirror) and is held together by knowledge (the key). The madhouse is man's hunger for the *serlo todo*—the freedom on which the *serse* is founded. The house of The Other, however, is also a house of death, for whether in society or in isolation man never achieves the total-being he desires and he ultimately dies.

There is a logic to the fact that the audience does not witness the death of The Other. This is the death both of his being-for-others, his objectivity, as well as the death of his being-for-itself, his subjectivity. It is also the annihilation of that profound freedom on which the *serse* is founded and which expresses itself as a hunger for being. To "know" this moment, the spectator himself would have to die.

In *The Other*, as in *No Exit*, a dead consciousness con-

tinues to exist as a being for the living. After he is gone, The
Other lingers on in the thoughts of the characters who remain
on stage. Damiana compares him to the "others" to whom she
is about to give birth and then states:

> The tomb is a cradle, and a cradle a tomb. It's what gives a man
> life so that he may dream it, for only dreams are life. And what
> gives man life gives death to an angel who was sleeping the terri-
> ble joy of eternity . . . eternal but empty. The cradle is a tomb.
> The maternal womb is a sepulcher. (p. 290)

Life begins in nothingness and ends in nothingness and is never
more than a dream of being. Though this is reminiscent of *Life
Is a Dream*, we are left without Calderón's ideal of a world
beyond the grave.

After the death of The Other, Don Juan, a character repre-
senting reason, wishes to pursue the mystery. The quixotic
Nurse, however, knows that reason, when carried to the limit,
can render only a knowledge of death. Her advice is that man
should, in spite of everything, dream of an ideal beyond the
limits of reason.

> Close your eyes to the mystery! It's the uncertainty of our su-
> preme hour which allows us to live at all, and it is the secret of
> our destiny, of our true personality, which allows us to dream. . . .
> Let us dream, then, and not seek a solution to the dream. (pp.
> 295–96)

The Nurse then speaks directly to the audience and to the
author, Unamuno. In a way similar to Augusto Pérez, she transcends the barriers separating the real from the fictional world.
She warns that the lives of the spectator and author, like those
of the characters, are mysteries which will end in death.

> The mystery! I don't know who I am, you don't know who you
> are, the teller of this story does not know who he is *(This last
> phrase may be changed to read "Unamuno does not know who
> he is.")*, and he doesn't know who any of those who listen to us
> may be. Every man dies, whenever Destiny arranges it, without
> ever having known himself. . . . (pp. 296–97)

Unamuno's *druma* thus represents a radical departure from traditional theater insofar as it posits as its goal not the enactment of roles but the destruction of roles. It is a theater which is conscious of itself as such and which undoes itself from within. When the character destroys the two dimensions of the *serse*, he unleashes man's profound freedom which hungers for the *serlo todo*. It is this freedom we discovered in Augusto Pérez and which, in Unamuno's ontology, lies at the heart of human reality. The Other, however, is a rebel whose rebellion leads nowhere but death. In the end we are left with a nothingness even more pervasive than the empty hell of *No Exit*. This leads us to the inevitable conclusion that man, according to Unamuno, is truly tragic.

Conclusions

In Contrast

Having articulated the thought of Unamuno and compared certain of his principal works of literature with those of Sartre, we are at last in a position to clarify the relationship between the two thinkers. Unamuno and Sartre share a fundamental intuition of human reality which they define in terms of tragedy. Yet their work has led us to different ends. To understand this situation, we must reconsider several of the basic premises of their thought.

The foundation of Sartre's entire philosophical enterprise is human freedom. It is through the ontological experiences of anguish, boredom, and nausea that freedom is revealed. In Unamuno the same experiences point not to freedom but to the limitations of the *serse*. Though a nothingness, man knows himself only through the Other. Freedom, therefore, could realize itself only in an ideal future when man is released from his present bondage and relieved of the tragic sense of life.

According to Sartre, historical man strives unceasingly to emancipate himself from the oppressive structures that alienate freedom, and for this reason his project is not only ontological but ethical. Because he is subject to the rule of scarcity, however, it is impossible for him at this time to envision a world in which freedom would be in full possession of itself. Nevertheless, Sartre contends that the means for achieving such a world are political and not spiritual.

Unamuno's ideal, on the other hand, does not involve a

change in the political structures of society nor the realization of socialism. Rather, it is immortality itself. Though experienced by the man of "flesh and blood," the tragic sense points not to the pain that results from hunger or material deprivation but to man himself as an absence of God. Unamuno's concerns are thus fundamentally religious.

Although Unamuno places the individual in opposition to society, he views the dispossessed not as the victims of an exploiting class but as mere creatures whose ignorance has spared them the anguish of living in a godless universe. He does not consider them a class nor do they, as in Sartre, ever realize reciprocity through revolutionary action. The only reciprocity they share is a function of their common faith in a god that Unamuno does not believe exists.

It follows that if through the bliss of ignorance the poor have remained unaware of their existential condition, they theoretically have nothing in common with Unamuno. What he calls the "select minority" is thus an aristocracy of the anguished. To be sure, both Unamuno and Sartre are bourgeois, but Sartre recognizes that the logical subject of the bourgeois intellectual's inquiries is the proletariat. He holds that the intellectual, regardless of his class, seeks the universal, and that only the proletariat can lay claim to the title of universal class. This is because the proletariat has posited freedom and the end of man's exploitation of man as its primary goal. "The true conflicts of our period," which Sartre found missing in Unamuno's articulation of the tragic sense of life, are thus conflicts of class.

The most explicit difference separating Unamuno and Sartre is to be found in their treatment of socialism. The two move in opposite directions with regard to it. For a moment their paths intersect in their similar efforts to re-emphasize the fundamental position of the individual within the dialectical process. Unamuno, however, eventually abandons socialism and strives to realize his ideal through a kind of existential literature. Sartre, in contrast, incorporates socialism into existentialism in an attempt to render intelligible both the personal and social dimensions of the human condition.

Underlying this reaction to socialism is a religious problem which characterizes the entire course of their careers. Unamuno, though unable to make the Kierkegaardian leap of faith, retains a nostalgia for God. Sartre chooses atheism. While it is Unamuno's hope that the tragedy of life will find a happy ending, Sartre simply lets the matter drop.

Future Perspectives

Though the Sartrean system has permitted the articulation of an existentialist Unamuno, this does not mean that Sartre can account for all the possible "Unamunos." Unamuno possessed certain philosophical intuitions which Sartre either failed to comprehend or chose to ignore. These intuitions could and should play a significant role in the creation of what might one day be called a post-Sartrean ontology. They involve, not surprisingly, a vision of being and nothingness and of being-for-others.

In Sartre, as we have seen, nothingness is defined as the internal negation of consciousness of the being of which it is conscious. This definition means that man is the great revealer of being, the creator of culture, history itself. It does not, however, account for the history of things. In the *Critique* Sartre states that a dialectic of things (dialectical materialism) is conceivable, but not at this moment in human history. How could man know internally the workings of a dialectic that lay outside of himself? He could not, unless he were bound to it through a common being.

Unamuno suggested such a common being in his discussion of "the nothingness of things and the nothingness of persons." For some critics, this use of the word "nothingness" was no more than a cryptic designation for God—the spirit that cannot be named which moves through men and things. Modern science, nonetheless, has corroborated the existence of a kind of nothingness of things. We know, for example, of anti-matter on the sub-atomic level and of black holes on the cosmic level. Moreover, we know that there is a history of the universe which in some way involves a relationship between its material being and the so-called nothingness which preceded the "big-bang." To be sure, Unamuno did not view the world with the hindsight of post-Einsteinian physics. He did, however, possess an intuition which science has verified and with which philosophy must come to terms if it is to achieve a total view of both the subjective and objective dimensions of reality.

Sartre and Unamuno also differ in their definition of being-for-others. According to Sartre, human relations are based not on a *Mitsein* but on conflict. This means that man can know the Other only in a relation of exteriority. Even in shame, he experiences the Other indirectly, through the realization of his own objectivity. It follows, then, that he knows only things. This, it might be said, is the great realism to which Sartre's atheism ultimately leads.

What, in fact, would a *Mitsein* be? A sort of mystical communion of nothingnesses? Such an ontological situation would certainly have been unacceptable to both Sartre's intellect and temperament. Nothingness, he knew, must be limited to consciousness or God would reappear in one form or another. A nothingness of things would amount to God the Father while a common nothingness of men would lead to the Holy Spirit.

In contrast to Sartre, Unamuno conceived of a knowledge of the Other based not on conflict but on harmony. This is perhaps a vestige of his Christian idealism. It is also an expression of a profound existential truth: I am and am not the Other. Though I may be separated from the Other by an infrangible barrier of being, I can never forget, despite a lifetime of exile, that I was born of the Other and that our common bond is one not only of spirit but of what Unamuno chose to call "flesh and blood." Existentialism, as a philosophy of commitment, must not lose sight of this fact, as contemporary man hovers on the brink of nuclear annihilation.

Notes

Preface

1. Jean-Paul Sartre, *Search for a Method,* trans. and with introd. Hazel E. Barnes (New York: Alfred A. Knopf, 1963), p. 19.

2. Ibid., p. 19.

3. Federico de Onís, "Tres cartas de Unamuno," *La Torre,* 35–36 (1961): 59.

4. Simone de Beauvoir, *La Force des choses* (Paris: Gallimard, 1963), p. 333.

5. Jean-Paul Sartre, *Cahiers pour une morale* (Paris: Gallimard, 1983), p. 25. My translation.

6. Jean-Paul Sartre, *Saint Genet: Actor and Martyr,* trans. Bernard Frechtman (New York: George Braziller, 1963), p. 599.

Chronology

1. In preparing the chronology on Sartre I have relied to a large extent on the work of Michel Contat and Michel Rybalka, comps., *The Writings of Jean-Paul Sartre,* Vol. 1. *A Bibliographical Life,* trans. Richard C. McCleary (Evanston: Northwestern University Press, 1974).

1. Life History

1. Sartre, *Saint Genet,* p. 584.

2. See Jean-Paul Sartre, *The Words,* trans. Bernard Frechtman (New York: George Braziller, 1964).

3. Susan Gruenheck, Oreste F. Pucciani, and Michel Rybalka, "An Interview with Jean-Paul Sartre," in *The Philosophy of Jean-Paul Sartre*, ed. Paul Arthur Schilpp, The Library of Living Philosophers, 16 (La Salle, Ill.: Open Court Publishing Company, 1981): 24.

4. Oreste F. Pucciani, "Sartre and Flaubert as Dialectic," in *Philosophy of Sartre*, ed. Schilpp, p. 501.

5. Oreste F. Pucciani, "Sartre, Ontology, and the Other," in *Hypatia: Essays in Classics, Comparative Literature, and Philosophy*, eds. William Calder III, Ulrich K. Goldsmith, and Phyllis B. Kenevan (Boulder: Colorado Associated University Press, 1985), pp. 151–67.

6. Gruenheck, et al., "Interview with Sartre," p. 13.

7. In Hugo Lijerón Alberdi, *Unamuno y la novela existencialista* (La Paz, Bolivia: Los Amigos del Libro, 1970), p. 21. My translation.

8. For the most complete discussion of the politics of the early Unamuno see Rafael Pérez de la Dehesa, *Política y sociedad en el primer Unamuno: 1894–1904* (Madrid: Ciencia Nueva, 1966).

9. In Lijerón Alberdi, *Unamuno y la novela existencialista*, p. 27. My translation.

10. In Margaret Thomas Rudd, *The Lone Heretic: A Biography of Miguel de Unamuno y Jugo*. Introd. Federico de Onís (Austin: University of Texas Press, 1963), p. 149.

11. Sartre, *Words*, p. 51.

12. The term *Mitsein* (being-with) is used by Heidegger to describe a profound being through which individual consciousnesses are united.

13. Sartre, *Words*, p. 191.

14. Miguel de Unamuno y Jugo, *Novela/Nivola*, trans. and with introd. Anthony Kerrigan, Bollingen Series, LXXXV.6 (Princeton: Princeton University Press, 1976): 384.

15. Sartre, *Words*, p. 163.

2. Philosophy

1. Cited in Contat and Rybalka, comps., *Writings of Sartre*, 1: 151.

2. Jean-Paul Sartre, *What Is Literature?* trans. Bernard Frechtman (New York: Philosophical Library, 1949), p. 215.

3. See Philip W. Silver, *Ortega as Phenomenologist: The Genesis of "Meditations on Quixote"* (New York: Columbia University Press, 1978).

4. Sartre places the preposition *"de"* (of) between parentheses so as not to make the self an object of consciousness. In English the problem can be avoided by the use of the expression "self-consciousness."

5. Jean-Paul Sartre, *The Psychology of Imagination*, trans. Bernard Frechtman (New York: Philosophical Library, 1948), p. 267.

6. Ibid, p. 281.

7. Jean-Paul Sartre, *Being and Nothingness: An Essay on Phenomenological Ontology*, trans. and with introd. Hazel E. Barnes (New York: Philosophical Library, 1956), p. lxi. All references to *Being and Nothingness* are taken from this edition and page numbers will be indicated in parentheses after the quote.

8. I will capitalize the term "In-itself" (as well as "For-itself" and "For-others") when it is used as a noun.

9. The most concrete example of facticity is the body.

10. Sartre explains that when consciousness attempts to constitute an "Us-Object," it imagines an absolute Other, which would be God.

11. In the *Critique* Sartre will expand this notion into the theory of the "practico-inert."

12. See Ronald Aronson, "Sartre's Turning Point: The Abandoned *Critique de la Raison Dialectique*, Volume Two," in *Philosophy of Sartre*, ed. Schilpp, pp. 685–707.

13. In this study the *"Critique"* will refer to the first volume of the *Critique of Dialectical Reason*.

14. See Hazel E. Barnes, "Sartre as Materialist," in *Philosophy of Sartre*, ed. Schilpp, pp. 661–84.

15. Jean-Paul Sartre, *Critique of Dialectical Reason I: Theory of Practical Ensembles*, trans. Alan Sheridan-Smith (London: Verso, 1976), p. 80. All references to the *Critique* are taken from this edition and page numbers will be indicated in parentheses after the quote.

16. See Miguel Cruz Hernández, "La misión socrática de don Miguel de Unamuno," *Cuadernos de la Cátedra Miguel de Unamuno*, 3 (1952): 41–53.

17. Miguel de Unamuno y Jugo, *The Agony of Christianity and Essays on Faith*, trans. Anthony Kerrigan, annotated by Martin Nozick and Anthony Kerrigan, Bollingen Series, LXXXV.5 (Princeton: Princeton University Press, 1974), p. 216.

18. Ibid., p. 216.

19. Miguel de Unamuno y Jugo, *Obras Completas* (Madrid: Afrodisio Aguado, 1958–1964), 3:762. Henceforth all references to the *Obras Completas* of Afrodisio Aguado will be indicated by the letter "A" after the volume number. The translations will be mine.

20. Unamuno, *Agony*, p. 100.

21. Miguel de Unamuno y Jugo, *The Tragic Sense of Life in Men and Nations*, trans. Anthony Kerrigan, introd. Salvador de Madariaga, afterword William Barrett, Bollingen Series, LXXXV.4 (Princeton: Princeton University Press, 1972), pp. 151–52.

22. Ibid., p. 22.

23. The word *congoja* differs from the word *angustia* (anguish) insofar as it denotes an almost physical suffering. As we shall see in his novel, Unamuno locates consciousness not only in the mind but in the heart and body. An awareness of this consciousness, therefore, is not a psychological experience but an experience of the whole man.

24. Unamuno, *Tragic Sense of Life*, p. 21.

25. François Meyer, *L'Ontologie de Miguel de Unamuno* (Paris: Presses Universitaires de France, 1955), p. 16. My translation.

26. Blaise Pascal, *Pensées et opuscules*, ed. Léon Brunschvicg (Paris: Hachette, 1923), p. 350. My translation.

27. Antonio Sánchez Barbudo, "The Faith of Unamuno: His Unpublished Diary," *The Texas Quarterly*, 8 (Spring 1965): 57.

28. Unamuno, *Novela/Nivola*, p. 409.

29. Unamuno, *Obras Completas*, 1A, p. 167.

30. Unamuno, *Novela/Nivola*, pp. 453–54. See Paul R. Olson, "Unamuno's Lacquered Boxes: *Cómo se hace una no-*

vela and the Ontology of Writing," *Revista Hispánica Moderna*, 36 (1970–1971): 186–99.

31. Meyer, *L'Ontologie*, p. 52. My translation.

32. Sartre, *Being and Nothingness*, p. xlvi.

33. *"Serse"* is a reflexive form of the verb *"ser"* (to be). It might be translated "to be oneself" or "self-being."

34. Unamuno, *Obras Completas*, 5A, p. 1192.

35. Ibid., 5A, pp. 1192–93.

36. Carlos Blanco Aguinaga, "'Authenticity' and the Image," in *Unamuno: Creator and Creation*, eds. José Rubia Barcia and M. A. Zeitlin (Berkeley and Los Angeles: University of California Press, 1967), p. 67.

37. Unamuno, *Obras Completas*, 3A, p. 427.

38. See Manuel Pizán, *Los hegelianos en España y otras notas críticas* (Madrid: Cuadernos para el diálogo, 1973), p. 30; and Antonio Regalado García, *El siervo y el señor: La dialéctica agónica de Miguel de Unamuno* (Madrid: Gredos, 1968), pp. 196–97.

39. Unamuno, *Obras Completas*, 5A, p. 1193.

40. *"Serlo todo"* is the opposite of *"serse."* It might be translated "to be it all" or "total-being."

41. For an important discussion of the conflict between consciousnesses in the world of Unamuno see Leon Livingstone, "The Novel as Self-Creation," in *Unamuno: Creator and Creation*, pp. 92–115.

42. Unamuno, *Agony*, p. 35.

43. Unamuno, *Obras Completas*, 3A, pp. 428–29.

44. Ibid., 3A, p. 433.

45. Ibid., 3A, p. 703.

46. Ibid., 3A, p. 705.

47. Ibid., 3A, pp. 705–706.

48. Unamuno, *Agony*, p. 167.

49. Ibid., p. 168.

50. Unamuno, *Novela/Nivola*, p. 429.

51. Miguel de Unamuno y Jugo, *Obras Completas* (Madrid: Escelicer, 1966–1971), 9: 481. Henceforth all references to the *Obras Completas* of Escelicer will be indicated by the letter "E" after the volume number. The translations will be mine.

52. Unamuno, *Obras Completas*, 9E, p. 477.

53. Ibid., 9E, pp. 1550–51.

54. Ibid., 9E, p. 1553.

55. Ibid., 9E, p. 1553.

56. Unamuno, *Obras Completas*, 3A, p. 472.

57. Ibid., 3A, p. 472.

58. Ibid., 3A, p. 473.

59. Ibid., 3A, pp. 475–76.

60. Ibid., 3A, p. 478.

61. Ibid., 3A, p. 898.

62. Unamuno, *Obras Completas*, 5A, pp. 1142–43.

63. Ibid., 3A, p. 758.

64. Meyer, *L'Ontologie*, p. 56. My translation.

65. Ibid., p. 56. My translation.

66. Sánchez Barbudo, "Faith of Unamuno," p. 46.

67. Regalado García, *El siervo y el señor*, pp. 128–29. My translation.

68. Unamuno, *Obras Completas*, 3A, p. 764.

3. Literary Theory

1. Sartre, *What Is Literature?*, pp. 11–12.

2. Ibid., p. 20.

3. Ibid., p. 24.

4. Ibid., p. 21.

5. Ibid., p. 39.

6. See Oreste F. Pucciani, "Cet Objet Sartrien Neuf: Un Centre Réel et Permanent d'Irréalisation," *Dalhousie French Studies*, 5 (1983): 90.

7. Sartre, *What Is Literature?*, p. 59.

8. Ibid., p. 65.

9. Ibid., pp. 62–63.

10. Ibid., p. 271.

11. Ibid., p. 276.

12. Jean-Paul Sartre, *L'Idiot de la famille* (Paris: Gallimard, 1971), 1:785–86, trans. Oreste F. Pucciani in "Sartre and Flaubert as Dialectic," in *Philosophy of Sartre*, ed. Schilpp, pp. 532–33.

13. Because Flaubert creates a "poetic prose," we realize

that there exists a third area of literature, located between pure poetry and pure prose. When interviewed by Pucciani, Sartre recognized the difficulties inherent in his theory of poetry and prose. See Gruenheck et al., "Interview with Sartre," in *Philosophy of Sartre*, ed. Schilpp, pp. 16–17.

14. Sartre, *Words*, p. 178.

15. Unamuno, *Novela/Nivola*, p. 422.

16. This understanding of poetry might be traced to childhood experiences. While Flaubert was constituted as an object by the members of his family, Unamuno experienced a profound freedom in his relationship with his father.

17. Unamuno writes in *Agony:* "Agony . . . means struggle. He who lives in the throes of struggle, struggling against life itself, lives in agony, agonizes." In Unamuno, *Agony*, p. 5.

18. Unamuno, *Novela/Nivola*, p. 411.

19. Unamuno, *Obras Completas*, 3A, p. 764.

20. Ibid., 11A, p. 675.

21. Ibid., 11A, p. 675.

22. Ibid., 16A, p. 384.

4. Novel

1. Simone de Beauvoir, "Littérature et métaphysique," *Les Temps Modernes*, 7 (April 1946): 1153–63.

2. Julián Marías Aguilera, *Miguel de Unamuno* (Madrid: Espasa-Calpe, 1943), p. 73. For further important discussion of the novel of Unamuno see Francisco Ayala, "Filosofía y novela en Unamuno," in *Spanish Thought and Letters in the Twentieth Century*, eds. Germán Bleiberg and E. Inman Fox (Nashville: Vanderbilt University Press, 1966), pp. 63–73; and Demetrios Basdekis, *Unamuno and the Novel*, University of North Carolina, Estudios de Hispanófila, 31 (Madrid: Castalia, 1974).

3. See Unamuno, *Obras Completas*, 2A, p. 334.

4. Marías Aguilera, *Miguel de Unamuno*, pp. 39–64.

5. Beauvoir, *La Force des choses*, p. 214.

6. Sartre, *Being and Nothingness*, p. 338.

7. Jean-Paul Sartre, *Nausea*, trans. Lloyd Alexander, introd. Hayden Carruth (New York: New Directions Publishing

Corp., 1964), p. 126. All references to *Nausea* are taken from this edition and page numbers will be indicated in parentheses after the quote.

8. Sartre, *Words*, p. 167.

9. Unamuno, *Novela/Nivola*, p. 27. All references to *Mist* are taken from this edition and page numbers will be indicated in parentheses after the quote.

10. Alexander A. Parker, "On the Interpretation of *Niebla*," in *Unamuno: Creator and Creation*, eds. Rubia Barcia and Zeitlin, pp. 116–38.

11. In the original: *"Y además me pareces otra."* ("And besides, you seem to me other.")

5. Theater

1. Jean-Paul Sartre, *Sartre on Theater*. Documents assembled, edited, introduced, and annotated by Michel Contat and Michel Rybalka, trans. Fred Jellinek (New York: Pantheon Books, 1976), p. 4.

2. Unamuno, *Obras Completas*, 12A, pp. 612–13.

3. Jean-Paul Sartre, *No Exit and Three Other Plays*, trans. Stuart Gilbert and Lionel Abel (New York: Vintage Books, 1961), p. 47. All references to *No Exit* are taken from this edition and page numbers will be indicated in parentheses after the quotes.

4. Sartre, *Being and Nothingness*, p. 540.

5. Ibid., p. 543.

6. Ibid., p. 494.

7. Ibid., pp. 607–609.

8. Ibid., p. 611.

9. Jean-Paul Sartre, preface to *Portrait of a Man Unknown: A Novel*, by Nathalie Sarraute, trans. Maria Jolas (New York: George Braziller, 1958), pp. vii–xiv. Sartre's description of the characters of Nathalie Sarraute is suggestive of Unamuno's understanding of man in society. He states that her characters are "unauthentic" to the extent that they have been reduced to the commonplace. Behind the wall of their unauthenticity, however, lies nothing.

10. Henceforth "The Other" will refer to the character of

the play while "the Other" to the being of existential ontology.

11. Miguel de Unamuno y Jugo, *Ficciones: Four Stories and a Play*, trans. Anthony Kerrigan, introd. and notes, Martin Nozick, Bollingen Series, LXXXV.7 (Princeton: Princeton University Press, 1976), pp. 257–58. All references to *The Other* are taken from this edition and page numbers will be indicated in parentheses after the quote.

12. In ontological terms, Cain's murder of Abel is motivated by what might be called "existential envy." As the object of God's love, Abel has achieved a fullness of being, while as the object of His indifference, Cain has experienced the anguish of nothingness. Cain envies the being which Abel possesses and which he lacks. The murder is thus an attempt on his part to become an object for God and thereby to achieve a fullness of being.

In Genesis the absolute Other through whom both the brothers discover themselves is God; in *The Other* it is society. Here, the murder represents an attempt on the part of the character to free himself from all objectification. It is motivated not by the anguish of nothingness but by the anguish of being other. Cf. José Rubia Barcia, "Unamuno the Man," in *Unamuno: Creator and Creation*, eds. Rubia Barcia and Zeitlin, p. 13; and Gregory L. Ulmer, *The Legend of Herostratus: Existential Envy in Rousseau and Unamuno* (Gainesville: University Presses of Florida, 1977).

13. Certain critics, such as Carlos Feal Deibe, have analyzed *The Other* in Freudian terms and have taken the house as a symbol of the character's conscious mind and the basement, where the body of the murdered brother is buried, as his unconscious mind. Rather than reiterate the various psychological interpretations, however, we have chosen to examine the characters in the light of Unamuno's own existential ontology. See Carlos Feal Deibe, *Unamuno: El Otro y don Juan* (Madrid: Cuspa, 1976).

Bibliography

Primary Sources

Sartre, Jean-Paul. *Being and Nothingness: An Essay on Phenomenological Ontology.* Translated and with introduction by Hazel E. Barnes. New York: Philosophical Library, 1956.

———. *Cahiers pour une morale.* Paris: Gallimard, 1983.

———. *Critique of Dialectical Reason I: Theory of Practical Ensembles.* Translated by Alan Sheridan-Smith. London: Verso, 1976.

———. *The Family Idiot: Gustave Flaubert: 1821–1857.* Vol. 1. Translated by Carol Cosman. Chicago: The University of Chicago Press, 1981.

———. *L'Idiot de la famille: Gustave Flaubert de 1821–1857.* Vols. 1–3. Paris: Gallimard, 1971–1972.

———. *Nausea.* Translated by Lloyd Alexander. Introduction by Hayden Carruth. New York: New Directions Publishing Corp., 1964.

———. *No Exit and Three Other Plays.* Translated by Stuart Gilbert and Lionel Abel. New York: Vintage Books, 1961.

———. Preface to *Portrait of a Man Unknown: A Novel.* By Nathalie Sarraute. Translated by Maria Jolas. New York: George Braziller, 1958.

———. *The Psychology of Imagination.* Translated by Bernard Frechtman. New York: Philosophical Library, 1948.

———. *The Roads to Freedom,* 3 vols. (1. *The Age of Reason.* Translated by Eric Sutton. 2. *The Reprieve.* Translated by

Eric Sutton. 3. *Troubled Sleep.* Translated by Gerard Hopkins.) New York: Alfred A. Knopf, 1947.

_____. *Saint Genet: Actor and Martyr.* Translated by Bernard Frechtman. New York: George Braziller, 1963.

_____. *Sartre on Theater.* Documents assembled, edited, introduced, and annotated by Michel Contat and Michel Rybalka. Translated by Fred Jellinek. New York: Pantheon Books, 1976.

_____. *Search for a Method.* Translated and with introduction by Hazel E. Barnes. New York: Alfred A. Knopf, 1963.

_____. *The Transcendence of the Ego: An Existentialist Theory of Consciousness.* Translated and with introduction by Forrest Williams and Robert Kirkpatrick. New York: Noonday Press, 1957.

_____. *What Is Literature?* Translated by Bernard Frechtman. New York: Philosophical Library, 1949.

_____. *The Words.* Translated by Bernard Frechtman. New York: George Braziller, 1964.

_____. *The Writings of Jean-Paul Sartre.* 2 vols. (1. *A Bibliographical Life.* 2. *Selected Prose.*) Compiled by Michel Contat and Michel Rybalka. Translated by Richard C. McCleary. Evanston: Northwestern University Press, 1974.

Unamuno y Jugo, Miguel de. *Cartas inéditas.* Compiled and with prologue by Sergio Fernández Larraín. Santiago de Chile: Zig-Zag, 1965.

_____. *Obras Completas.* Prologue, edition, and notes by Manuel García Blanco. 16 vols. Barcelaon: Vergara, 1958–1964. With special permission from Afrodisio Aguado.

_____. *Obras Completas.* Introductions, bibliographies, and notes by Manuel García Blanco. 9 vols. Madrid: Escelicer, 1966–1971.

_____. *Peace in War: A Novel.* Translated by Allen Lacy and Martin Nozick with Anthony Kerrigan. Annotated by Allen Lacy and Martin Nozick. Introduction by Allen Lacy. Bollingen Series, LXXXV.1. Princeton: Princeton University Press, 1983.

_____. *The Private World: Selections from the 'Diario Intimo' and Selected Letters: 1890–1936.* Translated by Anthony

Kerrigan, Allen Lacy, and Martin Nozick. Annotated by Martin Nozick with Allen Lacy. Introduction by Allen Lacy. Bollingen Series, LXXXV.2. Princeton: Princeton University Press, 1984.

——— . *Our Lord Don Quixote: The Life of Don Quixote and Sancho*. Translated by Anthony Kerrigan. Introduction by Walter Starkie. Bollingen Series, LXXXV.3. Princeton: Princeton University Press, 1967.

——— . *The Tragic Sense of Life in Men and Nations*. Translated by Anthony Kerrigan. Introduction by Salvador de Madariaga. Afterword by William Barrett. Bollingen Series, LXXXV.4. Princeton: Princeton University Press, 1972.

——— . *The Agony of Christianity and Essays on Faith*. Translated by Anthony Kerrigan. Annotated by Martin Nozick and Anthony Kerrigan. Bollingen Series, LXXXV.5. Princeton: Princeton University Press, 1974.

——— . *Novela/Nivola*. Translated and with introduction by Anthony Kerrigan. Bollingen Series, LXXXV.6. Princeton: Princeton University Press, 1976.

——— . *Ficciones: Four Stories and a Play*. Translated by Anthony Kerrigan. Introduction and notes by Martin Nozick. Bollingen Series, LXXXV.7. Princeton: Princeton University Press, 1976.

Secondary Sources

Abellán, José Luis. "Influencias filosóficas en Unamuno." *Insula*, 181 (1961): 11.

Abrams, Fred. "Sartre, Unamuno and the 'Hole Theory.'" *Romance Notes*, 5 (1963–1964): 6–11.

Alcalá, Angel. "Para 'otro' Unamuno a través de su teatro." *Papeles de Son Armadans*, 78 (1975): 217–43.

Alonso, José M. "Thematic Affinities in the Drama of Sartre and Unamuno: *Les Mouches* and *La Esfinge*." *Comparative Literature in Canada*, 4 (Spring 1972): 38.

Aronson, Ronald. "Sartre's Turning Point: The Abandoned *Critique de la Raison Dialectique*, Volume Two." In *The Philosophy of Jean-Paul Sartre*. Edited by Paul Arthur Schilpp.

The Library of Living Philosophers, 16. La Salle, Ill.: Open Court Publishing Company, 1981, pp. 685–707.

Ayala, Francisco. "Filosofía y novela en Unamuno." In *Spanish Thought and Letters in the Twentieth Century.* Edited by Germán Bleiberg and E. Inman Fox. Nashville: Vanderbilt University Press, 1966, pp. 63-73.

Azaola, José Miguel de. "Las cinco batallas de Unamuno contra la muerte." *Cuadernos de la Cátedra Miguel de Unamuno,* 2 (1951): 3–109.

———. "Unamuno et l'Existentialisme." *La Vie Intellectuelle,* 24 (1953): 31–49.

Barnes, Hazel E. "Sartre as Materialist." In *The Philosophy of Jean-Paul Sartre.* Edited by Paul Arthur Schilpp. The Library of Living Philosophers, 16. La Salle, Ill.: Open Court Publishing Company, 1981, pp. 661–84.

Basdekis, Demetrios. *Unamuno and the Novel.* University of North Carolina. Estudios de Hispanófila, 31. Madrid: Castalia, 1974.

Beauvoir, Simone de. *La Force des choses.* Paris: Gallimard, 1963.

———. "Littérature et métaphysique." *Les Temps Modernes,* 7 (April 1946): 1153–63.

Blanco Aguinaga, Carlos. "Aspectos dialécticos de las *Tres novelas ejemplares.*" *Revista de Occidente,* 19 (October 1964): 51–70.

———. "'Authenticity' and the Image." In *Unamuno: Creator and Creation.* Edited by José Rubia Barcia and M. A. Zeitlin. Berkeley and Los Angeles: University of California Press, 1967, pp. 48–71.

———. *El Unamuno contemplativo.* México: El Colegio de México, 1959.

———. "Interioridad y exterioridad en Unamuno." *Nueva Revista de Filología Hispánica,* 7 (1953): 686–701.

———. "Unamuno's 'yoísmo' and Its Relation to Traditional Spanish Individualism." Translated by George G. Wing. In *Unamuno: Centennial Studies.* Edited and with introduction by Ramón Martínez-López. Austin: University of Texas Press, 1966, pp. 18–52.

Borel, Jean Paul. *El teatro de lo imposible: Ensayo sobre una de las dimensiones fundamentales del teatro español contemporáneo.* Translated by Gonzalo Torrente Ballester. Madrid: Guadarrama, 1966.

Cantel, Raymond. "French Reactions to the Work of Unamuno." Translated by George Ayer. In *Unamuno: Centennial Studies.* Edited and with introduction by Ramón Martínez-López. Austin: University of Texas Press, 1966, pp. 53–72.

Cháves, Marcia C. "Unamuno: Existencialista cristiano." *Cuadernos de la Cátedra Miguel de Unamuno,* 22 (1972): 61–81.

Clavería, Carlos. *Temas de Unamuno.* Madrid: Gredos, 1953.

Collado, Jesús Antonio. "Unamuno y el existencialismo de Soren Kierkegaard." *Revista de la Universidad de Madrid,* 13 (1964): 145–61.

Cossío, José María de. *Miguel de Unamuno: Antología poética.* Buenos Aires: Espasa-Calpe, 1946.

Cruz Hernández, Miguel. "La dialectique du 'moi' et de 'l'autre' dans la pensée de Miguel de Unamuno." *L'Homme et Son Prochain: Actes du VIIIe Congrès des Sociétés de Philosophie de Langue Française.* Toulouse: Presses Universitaires de France, 1956, pp. 273–75.

———. "La misión socrática de don Miguel de Unamuno." *Cuadernos de la Cátedra Miguel de Unamuno,* 3 (1952): 41–53.

Egido, L. G. "Unamuno y Sartre." *Insula,* 226 (1965): 7.

Ehrenburg, Ilya. *Duhamel, Gide, Malraux, Mauriac, Morand, Romains, Unamuno, vus par un écrivain d'U.R.S.S.* Translated by Madeleine Etard. Paris: Gallimard, 1934.

Enjuto, Jorge. "Sobre la idea de la 'Nada' en Unamuno." *La Torre,* 35–36 (1961): 265–75.

Erro, Carlos Alberto. *Diálogo existencial.* Buenos Aires: Sur, 1937.

———. "Unamuno y Kierkegaard." *Sur,* 49 (October 1938): 7–21.

Fasel, Oscar A. "Observations on Unamuno and Kierkegaard." *Hispania,* 38 (1955): 443–50.

Feal Deibe, Carlos. *Unamuno: El Otro y don Juan.* Madrid: Cuspa, 1976.

Ferrater Mora, José. "On Miguel de Unamuno's Idea of Reality." *Philosophy and Phenomenological Research,* 21 (1960–1961): 514–20.

_____. *Unamuno: Bosquejo de una filosofía.* Buenos Aires: Sudamericana, 1957.

Franco, Andrés. *El teatro de Unamuno.* Madrid: Insula, 1971.

Frank, Rachel. "Unamuno: Existentialism and the Spanish Novel." *Accent,* 9 (Winter 1949): 80–88.

Galbis, Ignacio, R.M. *Unamuno: Tres personajes existencialistas.* Barcelona: Ediciones Hispam, 1975.

García Bacca, Juan David. *Nueve grandes filósofos contemporáneos, y sus temas,* 1. Caracas: Ministerio de Educación Nacional de Venezuela, 1947.

García Blanco, Manuel. *Don Miguel de Unamuno y sus poesías: Estudio y antología de textos poéticos no incluidos en sus libros.* Salamanca: University of Salamanca, 1954.

_____. "El escritor uruguayo Juan Zorrilla de San Martín y Unamuno." *Cuadernos Hispanoamericanos,* 58 (1954): 29–57.

_____. *En torno a Unamuno.* Madrid: Taurus, 1965.

_____. "Teixeira de pascoaes y Unamuno: Breve historia de una amistad." *Indice de Artes y Letras,* 79 (1955): 18–19.

González Caminero, N., R.P. "Miguel de Unamuno, precursor del existencialismo." *Pensamiento,* 5 (1949): 455–71.

_____. *Unamuno: Trayectoria de su ideología y su crisis religiosa.* Comillas: Universidad Pontificia, 1948.

Grau, Jacinto. *Unamuno, su tiempo y su España.* Buenos Aires: Alda, 1946.

Grene, Marjorie. *Introduction to Existentialism.* Chicago: The University of Chicago Press, 1968.

Gruenheck, Susan, Oreste F. Pucciani, and Michel Rybalka. "An Interview with Jean-Paul Sartre." In *The Philosophy of Jean-Paul Sartre.* Edited by Paul Arthur Schilpp. The Library of Living Philosophers, 16. La Salle, Ill.: Open Court Publishing Company, 1981, pp. 5–51.

Gullón, Ricardo. *Técnicas de Galdós.* Madrid: Taurus, 1970.

Guy, Alain. "Miguel de Unamuno: Pélerin de l'Absolu." *Cuadernos de la Cátedra Miguel de Unamuno,* 1 (1948): 75–102.

101

Horowitz, Renee B. "Cain and Abel as Existentialist Symbols for Unamuno and Hesse." *Papers on Language and Literature*, 16 (1980): 174–83.

Huarte Morton, Fernando. "El ideario lingüístico de Miguel de Unamuno." *Cuadernos de la Cátedra Miguel de Unamuno*, 5 (1954): 5–183.

Huertas Jourda, José. *The Existentialism of Miguel de Unamuno*. Gainesville: The University of Florida Press, 1963.

Ilie, Paul. *Unamuno: An Existential View of Self and Society.* Madison: University of Wisconsin Press, 1967.

———. "Unamuno, Gorky, and the Cain Myth: Toward a Theory of Personality." *Hispanic Review*, 29 (1961): 310–23.

Johnson, William D. "La antropología filosófica de Miguel de Unamuno: La conciencia y el sentimiento trágico de la vida." *Cuadernos de la Cátedra Miguel de Unamuno*, 20 (1970): 41–76.

———. "La palabra y el origen de la conciencia reflexiva en la filosofía de Miguel de Unamuno." *La Palabra y el Hombre: Revista Unamuniana de Veracruz*, 47 (July–September 1968): 411–23.

———. "Vida y ser en el pensamiento de Unamuno." *Cuadernos de la Cátedra Miguel de Unamuno*, 6 (1955): 9–50.

Kerrigan, Anthony. "Sorrow or Nothingness." *New Mexico Quarterly*, 24 (1954): 330–40.

Lacy, Allen. *Miguel de Unamuno: The Rhetoric of Existence.* The Hague and Paris: Mouton, 1967.

Larmeu, Pablo. "Unamuno y la novela ontológica." *Cuadernos Americanos*, 224 (1979): 217–31.

Lázaro, Fernando. "El teatro de Unamuno." *Cuadernos de la Cátedra Miguel de Unamuno*, 7 (1956): 5–29.

Levi, Albert W. "The Quixotic Quest for Being." *Ethics*, 66 (1956): 132–36.

Lijerón Alberdi, Hugo. *Unamuno y la novela existencialista.* La Paz, Bolivia: Los Amigos del Libro, 1970.

Livingstone, Leon. "The Novel as Self-Creation." In *Unamuno: Creator and Creation*. Edited by José Rubia Barcia and M. A. Zeitlin. Berkeley and Los Angeles: University of California Press, 1967, pp. 92–115.

MacGregor, Joaquín. "Dos precursores del existencialismo:

Kierkegaard y Unamuno." *Filosofía y Letras*, 22 (1951): 203–19.

Marías Aguilera, Julián. *El existencialismo en España: Presencia y ausencia*. Bogotá: Imprenta Nacional, 1953.

———. *Miguel de Unamuno*. Madrid: Espasa-Calpe, 1943.

Marrero Suárez, Vicente. *El Cristo de Unamuno*. Madrid: Rialp, 1960.

Martínez Blasco, Angel. "Existencialismo en la poesía de Unamuno." *Insula*, 181 (1961): 17.

Massini, Ferruccio. "L'esistenzialismo spagnolo di Unamuno (Cenni Tematici)." *Cuadernos de la Cátedra Miguel de Unamuno*, 6 (1955): 51–60.

Meyer, François. "Kierkegaard et Unamuno." *Revue de Littérature Comparée*, 29 (1955): 478–92.

———. *L'Ontologie de Miguel de Unamuno*. Paris: Presses Universitaires de France, 1955.

———. "Unamuno et les Philosophes." *Revista de la Universidad de Madrid*, 13 (1964): 77–92.

Molina, Ida. "Dialectics of the Search for Truth in *El Otro* and in *El tragaluz*." *Romantisches Jarbuch*, 24 (1973): 323–29.

Nozick, Martin. *Miguel de Unamuno*. New York: Twayne Publishers, 1971.

Olson, Paul R. "Unamuno's Lacquered Boxes: *Cómo se hace una novela* and the Ontology of Writing." *Revista Hispánica Moderna*, 36 (1970–1971): 186–99.

Onís, Federico de. "Tres cartas de Unamuno." *La Torre*, 35–36 (1961): 57–62.

Otero, C. P. "Unamuno and Cervantes." In *Unamuno: Creator and Creation*. Edited by José Rubia Barcia and M. A. Zeitlin. Berkeley and Los Angeles: University of California Press, 1967, pp. 171–87.

Palmer, D. D. "Unamuno's Don Quijote and Kierkegaard's Abraham." *Revista de Estudios Hispánicos*, 3 (1969): 295—312.

París, Carlos. "La inseguridad ontológica, clave del mundo de Unamuno." *Revista de la Universidad de Madrid*, 13 (1964): 93–123.

———. *Unamuno: Estructura de su mundo intelectual*. Barcelona: Ediciones Península, 1968.

103

Parker, Alexander A. "On the Interpretation of *Niebla.*" In *Unamuno: Creator and Creation.* Edited by José Rubia Barcia and M. A. Zeitlin. Berkeley and Los Angeles: University of California Press, 1967, pp. 116–38.

Pascal, Blaise. *Pensées et opuscules.* Edited by Léon Brunschvicg. Paris: Hachette, 1923.

Pauker, Eleanor K. "Kierkegaardian Dread and Despair in Unamuno's 'El que se enterró.'" *Cuadernos de la Cátedra Miguel de Unamuno,* 16–17 (1966–1967): 75–91.

Pérez de la Dehesa, Rafael. *Política y sociedad en el primer Unamuno: 1894–1904.* Madrid: Ciencia Nueva, 1966.

Pizán, Manuel. *El joven Unamuno: Influencia hegeliana y marxista.* Madrid: Ayuso, 1970.

———. *Los hegelianos en España y otras notas críticas.* Madrid: Cuadernos para el diálogo, 1973.

Pucciani, Oreste F. "Cet Objet Sartrien Neuf: Un Centre Réel et Permanent d'Irréalisation." *Dalhousie French Studies,* 5 (1983): 84–97.

———. "Jean-Paul Sartre." In *Histoire de la Philosophie,* 3. Encyclopédie de la Pléiade. Paris: Gallimard, 1971, pp. 641–91.

———. "Sartre and Flaubert as Dialectic." In *The Philosophy of Jean-Paul Sartre.* Edited by Paul Arthur Schilpp. The Library of Living Philosophers, 16. La Salle, Ill.: Open Court Publishing Company, 1981, pp. 495–538.

———. "Sartre, Ontology, and the Other." In *Hypatia: Essays in Classics, Comparative Literature, and Philosophy.* Edited by William Calder III, Ulrich K. Goldsmith, and Phyllis B. Kenevan. Boulder: Colorado Associated University Press, 1985, pp. 151–67.

Regalado García, Antonio. *El siervo y el señor: La dialéctica agónica de Miguel de Unamuno.* Madrid: Gredos, 1968.

Ribas, Pedro. "El Volkgeist de Hegel y la Intrahistoria de Unamuno." *Cuadernos de la Cátedra Miguel de Unamuno,* 21 (1971): 23–33.

Richards, Katherine C. "Unamuno and 'The Other.'" *Kentucky Romance Quarterly,* 23 (1976): 439–49.

Romero Flores, Hipólito. *Unamuno: Notas sobre la vida y la obra de un máximo español.* Madrid: Ediciones Hesperia, 1941.

Rubia Barcia, José. "Alonso Quijano y Don Quijote: Reflexiones sobre el 'ser' de la novela." *Cuadernos,* 47 (1961): 84–94.

———. "La Pardo Bazán y Unamuno." *Cuadernos Americanos,* 113 (1960): 240–63.

———. "Unamuno the Man." In *Unamuno: Creator and Creation.* Edited by José Rubia Barcia and M. A. Zeitlin. Berkeley and Los Angeles: University of California Press, 1967, pp. 4–25.

Rudd, Margaret Thomas. *The Lone Heretic: A Biography of Miguel de Unamuno y Jugo.* Introduction by Federico de Onís. Austin: University of Texas Press, 1963.

Sánchez Barbudo, Antonio. "El misterio de la personalidad en Unamuno." *Revista de la Universidad de Buenos Aires,* 15 (July–September 1950): 201–54.

———. "The Faith of Unamuno: His Unpublished Diary." *The Texas Quarterly,* 8 (Spring 1965): 46–66.

Sánchez Ruiz, José María. "Dimensión mundanal y social del ser según Unamuno." *Cuadernos de la Cátedra Miguel de Unamuno,* 12 (1962): 31–74.

Schürr, Friedrich. *Miguel de Unamuno: Der Dichterphilosoph des Tragischen Lebensgefühls.* Bern: Franke, 1962.

Schuster, Edward James. "Existentialist Resolution of Conflicts in Unamuno." *Kentucky Foreign Language Quarterly,* 8 (1961): 134–39.

Serrano Plaja, Arturo. "Náusea y niebla." *Revista de Occidente,* 26 (1969): 295–328.

Serrano Poncela, Segundo. "El Dasein heideggeriano en la generación del 98." *Sur,* 184 (1950): 35–57.

———. *El pensamiento de Unamuno.* México: Fondo de Cultura Económica, 1953.

Silver, Philip W. *Ortega as Phenomenologist: The Genesis of "Meditations on Quixote."* New York: Columbia University Press, 1978.

Stern, Alfred. "Unamuno: Pioneer of Existentialism." In *Unamuno: Creator and Creation.* Edited by José Rubia Barcia and M. A. Zeitlin. Berkeley and Los Angeles: University of California Press, 1967, pp. 26–47.

Tornos, Andrés M., S.J. "Sobre Unamuno y Kierkegaard." *Pensamiento*, 18 (1962): 131–46.

Torre, Guillermo de. "De Unamuno a Sartre." *Pro Arte* (Santiago de Chile), 3 (April 2, 1951).

——. "Unamuno y su teatro." *Papeles de Son Armadans*, 36 (January 1965): 13–44.

Ulmer, Gregory L. *The Legend of Herostratus: Existential Envy in Rousseau and Unamuno*. Gainesville: University Presses of Florida, 1977.

Valdés, Mario. "Observaciones unamunianas: Sobre la palabra del yo y del otro." *Revista de Occidente*, 13 (1966): 425–28.

Vivanco, Luis Felipe. *Introducción a la poesía española contemporánea*. Madrid: Guadarrama, 1957.

Young, Howard Thomas. *The Victorious Expression: A Study of Four Contemporary Spanish Poets: Miguel de Unamuno, Antonio Machado, Juan Ramón Jiménez, Federico García Lorca*. Madison: University of Wisconsin Press, 1964.

Zavala, Iris M. *Unamuno y su teatro de conciencia*. Salamanca: University of Salamanca, 1963.

Zubizarreta, Armando F. "Aparece un 'Diario inédito' de Unamuno." *Mercurio Peruano*, 28 (1952): 182–89.

——. "Una desconocida filosofía lógica de Unamuno." *Boletín Informativo del Seminario de Derecho Político de la Universidad de Salamanca*, 20–23 (1958): 241–52.

——. *Unamuno en su nivola*. Madrid: Taurus, 1960.

Index

literature, x; and the novel,
53; and philosophical inquiry,
x. *See also* Knowledge;
Language; Mist; Reason
Existentialism, x, xvii, 15, 53;
and commitment, 86; as
humanism, ix; vs. Marxism,
3, 20; as methodological
approach, ix, 3; and socialism,
84. *See also* Unamuno

Facticity, 14–15, 18, 55–56; as
body, 89 (n. 9); as limit-
situation, 70
Faith, 46, 84; as creative
imagination, 37. *See also*
Kierkegaard; Unamuno
Flaubert, Gustave, ix, xviii, xix,
3, 12, 19, 44–48, 50, 92–93
(n. 13), 93 (n. 16). *See also*
Poetic attitude; Sartre: *The
Family Idiot*
For-itself [(Being) For-itself], 14,
16–19, 28, 30, 36, 42, 44, 55,
62, 72, 74, 77, 79–80; as
consciousness, 14; as
contradictory, 14. *See also*
Aesthetic object; For-others;
Freedom; God; Knowledge;
Other, The; Poetry; *Serse*
For-others [(Being) For-others],
16–17, 21, 28–29, 44, 61, 71,
73–74, 77, 79–80, 85–86; and
Ego, 16; as For-itself, 16–17;
knowledge of, 17. *See also*
Death; *Ekstasis*; Ethics;
Language; Other, The; *Serse*
Franco, Francisco, xvi, 6
Freedom, 6, 12, 15–16, 22,
24–25, 31–32, 40–42, 48, 52,
57, 62, 66, 75–76, 83, 93
(n. 16); as condemnation, 75;
of consciousness, 12, 57; of

For-itself, 14; as hunger, 80,
82; and knowledge, 25; and
language, 8, 69; and love, 62;
and the Other, 75; and
philosophical inquiry, x, 10,
25; and proletariat, 84; and
Sartre, 10, 43, 83; and *serse,*
80; in theater vs. novel,
69–70; as truth, 24. *See also*
Aesthetic object; Bad faith;
Ethics; Literature; Other, The;
Poetry; Prose; Reader; *Serse;*
Writer/author

Garaudy, Roger, xviii
Genet, Jean, ix, xi, xvii, xviii,
12. *See also* Sartre: *Saint
Genet: Actor and Martyr*
God, 8, 25, 45, 47, 64, 67–68,
70, 79, 85–86; absence of, 19,
45, 84; death of, 5; as desire,
36–37; and immortality, 37; as
In-itself-For-itself, 18–19, 36,
40; as necessity, 58; as
nothingness, 85; as Other, 89
(n. 10), 95 (n. 12); as *serse/
serlo todo,* 36. *See also* Other,
The; Poetry
Good faith, 16; of prose writer,
39
Group-in-fusion, 19, 24
Guevara, Che, xix
Guillemin, Louise, xvi

Hegel, Georg, 4, 15, 28 29
Heidegger, Martin, xvi, 2, 88
(n. 12)
History, 19–24, 32–34, 85;
determinism of, 24, 43; as
expansion and contraction,
35; as hunger, 33; knowledge
of, 20; as man, 35, 85; as
spiral, 4; of things, 85. *See
also* Dialectic; Literature

Holy Spirit, 8, 86. *See also*
    Other, The
Husserl, Edmund, xvi, 2, 11

Idea: as form, 30; as language,
    30; as seriality, 30; vs. things,
    7; and tragic sense, 26. *See
    also* Matter
Idealism, x, 33; historical, 33.
    See also Christianity;
    Materialism; Sartre;
    Unamuno
Imaginary, The, 35, 37, 40, 46,
    48, 51–52, 54, 56–57, 59–60;
    as beautiful, 12; and
    contingency, 56. *See also*
    Reading; Writer/author
Imaginary object: as aesthetic
    object, 39–40; as poetry/prose,
    41
Imagination, 25; and art, 12–13;
    as creation, 35–36; as
    knowledge, 35–36; as
    language, 35; and the real, 12;
    and *serlo todo*, 36; and *serse*,
    36. *See also* Faith
In-itself [(Being) In-itself], 13–14,
    16, 18–19, 30, 32, 36, 39, 42,
    44, 55, 74; of consciousness,
    18; as fog, 57, 60; as
    nothingness, 28. *See also*
    Aesthetic object; Death; God;
    Knowledge; Poetry
Intentionality, 11, 31–32
Interest, 23

Kant, Immanuel, 27
Kierkegaard, Søren, x, xiv, 70;
    leap of faith, 85
Knowledge, 17, 20, 25, 30–32;
    and existence, x, 59; and
    name, 30; and necessity, 58;
    as penetration, 30, 62; as

relationship between
    consciousnesses, 30; as
    relationship between For-itself
    and In-itself, 14. *See also*
    Anguish; Dialectic; For-
    others; Freedom; History;
    Imagination; Language;
    Nothingness; Other, The;
    Serlo todo; Serse

Lacan, Jacques, 28
La Lucha de Clases, 4, 33
Language, 8, 25, 39; as
    alienation, 30–31, 49, 69; and
    consciousness, 39–40; and
    existence, 69; as For-others,
    17–18, 22, 46, 69; as
    knowledge, 17, 30; limitations
    of, x, 48; as relationship to
    Other, 18, 22–23, 30, 46; and
    serse, 49, 69. *See also*
    Freedom; Idea; Imagination;
    Practico-inert; Reason;
    Theater
Les Temps Modernes, xvii, xix
Literature, 10–11, 42, 48, 50; as
    aesthetic object, 38, 40; as
    death, 8, 48; demystification
    of, 45; and freedom, 41–42; as
    "historia," 64; Nobel Prize
    for, xv, xix; and philosophy,
    38; and *serse*, 48; and style,
    49; and truth, 32. *See also*
    Commitment; Ethics;
    Existence
Lizárraga, Concepción, xiii
Look, The, 16–17, 59, 62–63, 65,
    72–75
Love, 8, 36, 62, 65. *See also*
    Freedom

Machado, Manuel, 63
Maoism, xix

INDEX

(Poet, *continued*)
nothingness, 49; as political
activist, 47; and *serlo todo*,
37, 48; and *serse*, 48. *See also*
Tragic sense; Unamuno
Poetic attitude, 39; in Flaubert,
45–48; in Unamuno, 48
Poetry, 38–39, 44–45; and death,
49; as essence, 39–40; and
freedom, 41–42; and God, 40;
as In-itself-For-itself, 40, 42;
and style, 49; in Unamuno vs.
Sartre, 49–50. *See also*
Commitment; Imaginary
object
Positivism, 4, 20
Possibility, 18
Practico-inert, 19, 22–24,
31–32, 43, 45, 89 (n. 11); as
immaterial matter, 22, 42; as
language, 22–23; as practical
totality, 43. *See also* Aesthetic
object; Class; *Serse*
Praxis, 20, 22–24, 30, 43–44; as
need and labor, 21; mini-, 44
Primo de Rivera, Miguel, xv, 5,
48
Prose, 38–39, 44; as action, 39;
and freedom, 41–42; poetic,
92–93 (n. 13); as sign, 39. *See
also* Commitment; Good
faith; Imaginary object
Psyche, 11–12, 16, 28–29. See
also *Serse*
Pucciani, Oreste, 2–3, 92–93
(n. 13)

Reader, 39, 48; and aesthetic
object, 40–41; and character,
52, 54, 67–68; freedom of,
40–42, 68; as Other, 68. *See
also* Mist; Tragic sense;
Writer/author

Reading, 42, 48; and imaginary,
42; and Other, 42; as
perception and creation,
40–41
Real, The, 7–8, 35, 39, 45–47,
56–57; as contingent, 12; vs.
fictional, 64, 66–67, 81; as
non-intentional, 32; as Other,
32. *See also* Imagination;
Sartre
Reason, 50; and consciousness,
32; and death, 81; and
existence, 26; as language, 32;
and social being, 32. *See also*
Dialectical reason; Other, The
Reflective scissiparity, 11, 57
Regalado García, Antonio, 37
Regressive-progressive method:
as dialectical reason, 19; and
The Family Idiot, 19–20
Roosevelt, Franklin D., xvii

Sánchez Barbudo, Antonio, 37
Sarraute, Nathalie, 76
SARTRE, JEAN-PAUL: as atheist, 3,
8–9, 45, 85–86; childhood,
xvi, 1, 6–9; commitment of, 2,
47; and father-figure, xvi, 6–8;
idealism of, 1, 4, 7–8, 60; as
phenomenologist, 2; as realist,
x, 86; as student, xvi, 1–2;
war experience of, xvii, 2–3;
as writer, 1–2, 8–9, 45, 60. *See
also* Freedom; Poetry;
Tragedy; Tragic sense
—Works: *Being and
Nothingness*, xvii, 3, 10–19,
21–22, 24, 27–28, 36, 38, 40,
42, 45, 55, 72–73; *Cahiers
pour une morale*, xi, xviii,
xix; *Critique of Dialectical
Reason*, x, xviii, xix, 3–4,
10–11, 19–24, 29, 42–43, 45,

112

(Unamuno, continued)
Christian thinker, 27; exile of,
xv, 5, 48; as existentialist,
ix–xi, 5, 25–26, 84; faith of,
4–5, 7–8, 36–37; and father-
figure, xiii, 6–7, 93 (n. 16);
and fascism, xvi, 5–6; as
Hegelian, 4; idealism of, xiii,
6–7; phenomenologist, 27; as
poet, x, 47, 50; as precursor of
Sartre, xiv–x; as rector,
xiii–xvi, 5; religious crisis of,
xiii, 3–5; as socialist, xiii,
4–5, 32–33, 84; as student,
xiii, 4; as writer, 8–9, 38, 47.
See also Poetic attitude;
Poetry; Tragedy; Tragic sense
—Works: The Agony of
Christianity, xv, xvi, 6, 26, 30,
93 (n. 17); "Civilization and
Culture," 34–35; How to
Make a Novel, xv, 6–9, 27, 32,
47–49, 55; "The Idealist
Conception of History," 33;
"Ideocracy," xiv, 30;
"Intellectuality and

Spirituality," 30–31; The Life
of Don Quixote and Sancho,
xiv, 51, 66; Logical
Philosophy, xiii, 4; Love and
Education, xiv, 54; Mist, xiv,
57, 59–68; On the Tragic
Sense of Life, xiv, xvi, 6, 26;
The Other, xv, 71, 76–82;
"Plenitude of Plenitudes," 36;
St. Manuel Bueno, Martyr, xv,
51; Soledad, 70; "What Is
Truth?," 31–32

Value, 18, 46, 74. See also
Aesthetic object; Slime
Violence, 21–22

World War II, 2–3, 55
Writer/author, 39, 48; and
aesthetic object, 40; and
character, 54, 64–67; freedom
of, 40–41; and imaginary, 8;
and reader, 40–42, 68; and
serse/serlo todo, 68. See also
Commitment; Good faith;
Sartre; Unamuno

About the Author

Robert Richmond Ellis is Assistant Professor of Spanish, Occidental College, Los Angeles, California. He received his B.A. from Pomona College and his M.A. and Ph.D. from the University of California, Los Angeles.